SOCIAL SUICIDE

SOCIAL

SUICIDE

GEMMA HALLIDAY

HARPER TEEN
An Imprint of HarperCollinsPublishers

HarperTeen is an imprint of HarperCollins Publishers.

Social Suicide
address HarperCollins Children's Books, a division of HarperCollins
Publishers, 10 East 53rd Street, New York, NY 10022.
www.epicreads.com

Library of Congress Cataloging-in-Publication Data
Halliday, Gemma.
  Social suicide / by Gemma Halliday.
    p. cm.
  Sequel to: Deadly cool.
  Summary: "Hartley Featherstone's first big story for the school paper
takes an unexpected turn when she discovers the girl she's supposed to
interview dead in her swimming pool"— Provided by publisher.
  ISBN 978-0-06-200332-4
  [1. Mystery and detective stories. 2. Journalism—Fiction. 3. High
schools—Fiction. 4. Schools—Fiction.] I. Title.
PZ7.H15449Soc 2012   2011042111
[Fic]—dc23   CIP
                                                    AC

Typography by Torborg Davern
12 13 14 15 16   CG/RRDH   10 9 8 7 6 5 4 3 2 1
❖
First Edition

FOR ALL THE TEACHERS I'VE HAD.
I HOPE I DIDN'T TURN TOO MANY HAIRS GRAY.

ACKNOWLEDGMENTS

ALTHOUGH I GENERALLY WRITE ALONE, IN A CORNER OF A coffee shop, with my earbuds in so no one will bother me, there is actually a huge team of people without whom my words would never see the light of day, let alone a bookstore shelf. So I have to give a shout-out to them.

A huge thanks to my agent-awesome, Holly Root, for always having my back. Thank you to Erica Sussman, Tyler Infinger, and the rest of the incredibly talented editorial team at HarperTeen for all their hard work on this book. And a big thanks to the Romance Divas for being the bestest writing community on the planet.

Thanks to Nicky for being my go-to guy on all things teen, and for letting me steal him to be a character in this book. You rock.

And lastly, a huge thank-you to the teachers at the "real" version of Herbert Hoover High, where I went to school. It boggles my mind how anyone can spend that many hours in a classroom by choice and still have a smile. So thanks for the smiles, the hard work, and even for the homework. (Yeah, I said it. Crazy, huh?)

ONE

YOU HAD TO BE INCREDIBLY STUPID TO GET CAUGHT cheating in Mr. Tipkins's class, but then again, Sydney Sanders was known for being the only brunette *blonder* than Paris Hilton.

HOMECOMING QUEEN HOPEFUL SUSPENDED
FOR CHEATING ON TEST

I looked down at my headline for the *Herbert Hoover High Homepage*, our school's online newspaper. Usually our news ran the exciting gambit from the custodian retiring to a hair being found in the Tuesday Tacos in the cafeteria. So a cheating scandal was way huge. And I'd been surprised when our paper's editor, Chase Erikson, had assigned me the biggest story since the principal's car was tagged in the back parking lot. After all, I'd only been working on the *Homepage* for a short time, making me the resident newbie.

I had a bad feeling that this story was some sort of a test. Do well and I'd earn the respect of my fellow reporters as well as a certain editor with whom I had a complicated personal history. Fail and it was the cafeteria beat for me.

Clearly I was shooting for outcome number one.

I turned up the volume on my iPod in an effort to drown out the noise of the school paper's tiny workroom and put my fingers to the keyboard.

Herbert Hoover High Homecoming Queen nominee Sydney Sanders was discovered cheating on Tuesday's midterm in her precalculus class. Mr. Tipkins caught Sydney red-handed when he noticed the answers to the test painted on her fingernails. Apparently Sydney had incorporated the letters A, B, C, or D into the design painted on her fake nails in the exact order that the answers appeared on the test. After Sydney was caught, it quickly came to light that her best friend, Quinn Leslie, had used the answers to cheat on her test as well. Both girls are suspended from HHH while administrators investigate how the answers to the midterm got out. Sydney, previously considered a front-runner in the upcoming elections, will no longer be eligible to be Herbert Hoover High's Homecoming Queen at next Saturday's dance.

"That the cheating story?" Chase asked, suddenly behind me.

Very close behind me.

I cleared my throat as the scent of fresh soap and fabric softener filled my personal space. I pulled out one earbud and answered, "Yeah. It is."

He was quiet for a moment reading my laptop screen over my shoulder. I felt nerves gathering in my belly as I waited for his reaction.

Chase Erikson was the reason I'd joined the school paper in the first place. He and I had both been investigating a murder at our school, each for different reasons. Chase because he was all about a hot story. And me because the murdered girl had been the president of the Chastity Club and had just happened to be sleeping with my boyfriend. Needless to say, he was now totally an ex-boyfriend. Anyway, Chase and I had sort of teamed up to find the Chastity Club killer, and once we did, Chase told me that I showed promising investigative skills and offered me a position on staff. Considering my college résumé was in need of some padding, I agreed.

So far working on the paper was a lot more fun than I

had anticipated. When I'd first heard the term *school paper* I'd envisioned a bunch of extra-credit-hungry geeks with newsprint-stained fingers. But in reality, the entire paper operated online—no newsprint—and several students I knew contributed—none of them geeks. Ashley Stannic did a gossip column once a week that was total LOLs, even if only half the rumors she printed were true. Chris Fret contributed sports commentary and kept a running poll on this semester's favorite player. In fact, the only thing that hadn't been all smiley faces about working at the paper so far was Chase himself.

Chase was tall, broad-shouldered, and built like an athlete. His hair was black, short, and spiky on top, gelled into the perfect tousled style. His eyes were dark and usually twinkling with a look that said he knew a really good secret no one else was in on. He almost always wore black, menacing boots and lots of leather.

One time Mom picked me up from the paper for a dentist appointment and, when she met Chase, described him as "a little rough around the edges." When Ashley Stannic played truth or dare at Jessica Hanson's sweet sixteen and had been pressed to tell the truth, she'd described Chase as "sex in a pair of jeans." Me? I wasn't quite sure what I thought of Chase. All I knew was that things had been uncomfortable and a little awkward between us since The Kiss.

Yes. I, Hartley Grace Featherstone, had swapped spit with HHH's resident Bad Boy.

When we'd worked together on that first story, I'd ended up getting kidnapped and almost killed. Almost, because Chase had been there to save me at the last minute. And as soon as Chase had rescued me, he'd kissed me.

Briefly. In the heat of the moment. When emotions were running high.

It was a night neither of us had spoken of since, and I was 99 percent sure that it had meant nothing at all beyond relief on both our parts that I was still alive.

But that other 1 percent still persisted just enough that in situations like this—where the scent of his fabric softener was making me lean in so close that I could feel the heat from his body on my cheek—I still wasn't sure whether I thought of Chase as sex in a pair of jeans or a guy who was a little rough around the edges.

"This is good," Chase said, bringing me back to the present.

"Thanks." I felt myself grinning at his praise.

"But you can do better."

And just like that, my grin dropped like a football player's GPA. "I can?"

Chase nodded. "Sydney got caught cheating yesterday. You really think there's any info in this article that every person on campus doesn't already know by now?"

I bit my lip. He was right. Within minutes of Sydney being busted, I'd personally received no less than twenty-five texts about it.

"So I should scrap the article?"

"No. Like I said, this is good. But you need more. You need to tell our readers something they don't know."

"Such as?"

"How did Sydney and Quinn get the answers to the test?"

I shrugged. "I dunno."

Chase straightened up, crossed his arms over his broad chest (covered today in a black T-shirt with a band logo featuring a bloody zombie corpse), and furrowed his eyebrows as he stared down at me. "'I dunno' is not in a good reporter's vocabulary."

"No one knows," I countered. "Quinn's not talking, and no one's seen Sydney since she was suspended."

"Someone must know something. Who else have you talked to?" he asked.

I picked up the purple notebook where I kept all my important notes. "I texted Sydney's boyfriend, Connor Crane, but he said all he knows is that Sydney is grounded for the rest of her life. And I saw the vice principal yesterday after school, and she said both Sydney and Quinn are suspended for the rest of the week."

"And?"

"And the administration is considering a dress code that applies to fake nails."

"And?"

"And I'm interviewing Mr. Tipkins tomorrow at lunch."

"And what do you plan to ask him?" Chase asked, arms still crossed as he towered over me.

I pursed my lips together. This was part of the test. I could feel it. "He caught Sydney. I thought his perspective might be interesting."

"Ahnt. Wrong."

I opened my mouth to defend my answer, but Chase was faster.

"His perspective isn't news. The facts are. Ask him how the answers to his test got out. Ask him where he keeps them, did Sydney or Quinn have access, how often does he reuse the same tests? Ask him how—"

"Okay, I get the point! Geez."

The right corner of Chase's lip curled up. "Good. I have faith you may make it as an actual reporter some day," he said. "Now go, young grasshopper. Make me proud."

And then he patted me on the head and walked away.

Actually patted me. Like one might pat his cocker spaniel.

Clearly this story was one test I seriously needed to pass if I was going to command any respect at the *Homepage*.

* * *

As soon as Chase left me to go proof Chris Fret's account of last Friday's football game, I made a list of questions to ask Mr. Tipkins. Then I packed up my stuff and headed out to the west field to catch a ride home with my best friend, Samantha Kramer, after her lacrosse practice.

Sam was on the field holding a long wooden stick with a basket-looking thing at one end to catch the ball. Which, unfortunately, was nowhere near Sam. She jogged down the field, looking winded, a good three yards behind the pack of other girls in black and orange HHH jerseys.

I felt for her. Sam was smart, sweet, and pretty much the friendliest person I knew. When I'd moved here from Southern California in fifth grade, I'd been terrified of going to a new school. That first day, Sam had accosted me at recess, insisted I join her and her friends on the monkey bars, and generally stuck to me like glue the entire week. I had never been more grateful for anyone in my entire life, and we'd been chained at the hip ever since. Sam was like the sister I never had.

But as much as I loved my pseudo-sister, I was the first to admit that Sam wasn't what you'd call naturally athletic. Or coordinated. In seventh grade she and I had joined the track team together, thinking the extra exercise might help shed a couple after-Christmas pounds. Sam had ended up taking out three wooden barriers in the hurdles race, two other racers in the 50-meter sprint, and the other team's coach in the discus throw. I'd ended up consoling her over her thwarted track career with a pint of Ben & Jerry's.

Which is why I had to think that lacrosse was a bit of a disaster in the making. It was only a matter of time before Sam either (A) broke a bone or (B) broke someone else's bone.

The coach blew a whistle, signaling a break, and I waved at Sam. She jogged over, looking immensely grateful for the rest.

"Whoever invented this game is insane," she panted. "Seriously, it's like hockey and basketball's painful love child." She reached down, rubbing at a bruise on her shin.

"At least you're looking better out there," I said. A stretch, but I was trying to be encouraging.

"You're such a liar," she said, leaning heavily on her stick. "But thanks."

"At least it's good exercise?" I said, trying again at the encouraging thing.

"Pft," she said, blowing air up at her forehead. "I'd rather run a billion miles on a treadmill."

"Why don't you just quit?"

"Because my dad says I need a sport on my résumé or Stanford won't let me in."

Sam's dad had been a Stanford man, as had his dad, and *his* dad. All hopes of carrying on the family tradition had previously been pinned on Sam's older brother, Kevin, until he'd dropped out of prelaw to join Greenpeace. Kevin now spent his days outside Whole Foods petitioning shoppers to save endangered animals, which meant that Sam was her father's only hope of having a Kramer of this generation graduate from Stanford.

"Can I bum a ride home with you?"

"Sure," she said. "My dad's picking me up after practice. Were you working late on the paper?"

I nodded. "I'm writing an article about Sydney Sanders. She got suspended yesterday."

"I heard. She and Quinn were both on the team. We're totally short without them."

"Do you know Sydney well?"

Sam shrugged. "Not really. Did you hear she got kicked off the homecoming court when she got caught?"

"Yeah. You don't have her number, do you?" I asked, thinking an interview with Sydney would be just the angle I needed to rock Chase's journalist world.

"Sure, but it won't do you any good. Her parents freaked when she got suspended and grounded her for pretty much her natural life. They took her phone, too."

Damn. There went that idea.

"But," Sam said.

"Yeah?"

"She still has her laptop, and she's been on Twitter.

Jessica Hanson said that Sydney tweeted during third period that she was bored out of her mind."

Perfect. I made a mental note to look her up as soon as I got home.

"Kramer!" a dark-haired girl across the field called to Sam. "Let's go!"

Sam sighed deeply. "I gotta go get beat up again."

"Knock 'em dead, killer," I said, taking a seat on the bleachers to wait while Sam jogged away, waving her lacrosse stick in a way that made me totally glad I was not on the opposing team. Or our team, for that matter.

An hour later, Sam's dad dropped me off in front of my house, and I walked up the front pathway to find the door unlocked, a sure sign Mom had beat me there.

I was ten when my mom and dad had finally decided to call it quits and get divorced. Dad had stayed behind in Los Angeles, and Mom had decided to move north to Silicon Valley, where she could put her programming degree to use, meaning she could work part-time from the house. Most of the time, I had to admit it was actually kinda nice to come home to someone.

Most of the time.

"Hartley," Mom called from the kitchen. "That you?"

"Yep," I responded, shutting the door behind me

"Come here for a sec."

I wandered toward the sound of her voice and found Mom on her laptop at the kitchen table. She was wearing her usual uniform of yoga pants, T-shirt, and Nikes, her hair twisted up into a messy sort of bun at the base of her neck, and peering at the screen through a pair of hot pink computer glasses. On the table next to her was a glass of green juice. Mom was a gluten-free, sugar-free vegan who didn't believe in preservatives of any kind. Which left two options for what she was drinking—celery or lawn trimmings.

"What's up?" I asked, standing next to her. I sniffed at her glass. If I had to guess? Lawn trimmings.

"I'm trying to upload a picture, but it's not working. I keep getting some kind of error. Help?"

Mom was a whiz with computer programming code. How she could come up with a string of letters and numbers that told a computer what to do, I had no idea. But she was hopeless when it came to user interface. She almost drove me insane when I was trying to get her set up on FarmVille.

I peeked over her shoulder at the screen. "What's the photo?"

She clicked a file icon and a younger version of her in a bright, poofy pink dress appeared on the screen.

"Dude." I think I actually physically shuddered.

"What?"

I gave her a look. "What is that?"

"My senior prom dress," she said.

"You look like a cupcake."

"It was the nineties," she said, giving me a playful swat on the shoulder. "Give me a break. That was cool then."

"And why are you uploading this monstrosity?"

Mom shot me a look over the top of her computer glasses. "I'm uploading this very flattering picture of myself because I need a profile photo."

"What are you making a profile for?"

Mom bit her lip. "An online site."

"What kind of site?"

"Just . . . a site."

I gave her a look. "Mom. What are you doing?"

She sighed. "Match dot com, okay? I'm making a profile on an online dating site."

"Mom!"

"What?" she asked, blinking in mock innocence. "Lots of people are on Match."

"Lots of weirdos."

"Lots of perfectly normal single people."

"Seriously, Mom, why would you want to go out with any of those people?"

"Why not? Hartley, it's been years."

"Years since what?"

Mom opened her mouth to speak, but I quickly changed my mind.

"Wait—don't answer that."

Okay, I'm not stupid. I know where babies come from and I know at some point my mother and father had to have done the deed in order for me to be here. Since then, though, Mom and Dad had divorced and moved three hundred miles away from each other, and the idea of sex and my parents had been a blissfully distant one.

Until now.

"You know what a lot of people your age do to fill their time?" I asked. "Hobbies. You could take up gardening or painting. Or knitting," I suggested.

Mom shot me a look. "Knitting? Exactly how old do you think I am, Hartley?"

"What? Lots of people knit. It's a great way to pass the time."

Mom shook her head. "Look, I'm not saying I'm ready to get married or jump into anything serious, hon. But I would like to get out and meet some people my own age. Okay?"

"Some men, you mean."

"Yes."

I looked from Mom to the photo. Well, on the upside, at least with this as her first impression, she wasn't likely to get too many offers.

Once I helped Mom upload her profile photo to Match.com (Though I drew the line at helping her come up with a "flirty" headline. Shudder.), I escaped to my room, and logged on to Twitter. I quickly found Sydney Sanders's page and DMed her saying I was doing an article for the school paper and wanted to get her side of the story. Then, while I waited to hear back, I scrolled through her most recent tweets. Apparently being grounded gave her a lot of free time, as there were at least a dozen an hour.

It also appeared, as I read them, that being grounded forever was really depressing. Each tweet was sadder than the last, starting out that morning with:

my life sux.

To that afternoon where she'd disintegrated to:

i have nothing left 2 live 4.

Drama much? Then again, Sydney did thrive on school social events like homecoming, and she had been in the running for queen, so maybe her life really was suckish to extreme.

An hour later I was still waiting for a response and was beginning to fear that maybe Sydney's parents had decided to take away her laptop, too. I was just about to give up and see what kind of vegan dinner I could beg out of my mom when a reply finally popped into my box. I clicked it.

what do u want to know?

Yes! I quickly typed back:

how did u get the cheats 2 the test?

A moment later her reply came in.

can't say.

Crap. Though honestly, if she hadn't told the vice principal how she got the answers under threat of losing the homecoming title, I knew the chances she'd tell me were slim. Still . . .

i want 2 print ur side of things. it's unfair u were suspended. u deserved to be hc queen.

This time there was no pause.

i know! totally unfair!

can we meet? 2morrow?

i'm grounded.

This I knew. But I also knew that Sydney lived on Teakwood Court, which backed up to the Los Gatos Creek biking trail. Conducting an interview through her back fence wasn't totally ideal, but if I met her there after school, at least it meant she wouldn't have to breach her grounding perimeter.

I typed my plan to her, and almost immediately I got a reply.

k. c u then.

I grinned. Now that was what even Chase would have to call real reporting.

TWO

THE NEXT DAY, I WAS SO ANTSY TO TELL SAM ABOUT MY meeting that as soon as the fourth-period bell rang, I dashed toward the cafeteria. Stacks of trays and cartons of chocolate milk lined one wall, while rows of tables and benches filled the room. The floors were gray linoleum, the walls dull beige, and posters advertising our upcoming homecoming dance were plastered over every available space. I grabbed my tray, loaded up on pizza sticks, an apple, and a carton of milk, and quickly found Sam sitting near the back of the cafeteria with her boyfriend, Kyle Lowe.

I hesitated.

Okay, here's the thing: I like Kyle fine. He's a cool guy. I totally have nothing against him. But lately something was happening to Sam whenever she was around him. She was turning from a normal, rational, sixteen-year-old girl into a cartoon character with little pink hearts floating out of her eyes. Suddenly she was saying things like "my wittle wuv" and "I gots to has you," getting so cutesy and grammatically incorrect it verged on embarrassing. I had yet to find a kind way to tell her this whole lovey-dovey thing was getting out of control.

Sam looked up, saw me contemplating my seating options, and waved me over.

Then turned to Kyle and gave him an Eskimo kiss with her nose.

Oh boy.

I made my way to their table and plopped my tray down, trying not to look as Kyle Eskimo kissed her right back.

"Look what I made us," Sam said right away, shoving her wrist toward me. On it was a pink friendship bracelet made of braided thread. In the middle was a pattern of a red heart.

"Very cute," I said.

"I made Kyle one, too," she told me, pulling his wrist out for inspection along with hers. "See? We match."

"Very . . . matchy."

She grinned. "Thanks."

I loved her enough that I didn't tell her it wasn't exactly a compliment.

"So, did you get ahold of Sydney last night?" Sam asked.

I nodded, digging into my pizza sticks. "Yeah. I'm meeting her after school."

"Meeting who?"

Chase suddenly appeared at my side, dropped a tray on the table, and straddled the bench next to me.

"What?" I asked innocently.

"Who are you meeting?"

I paused. Truth was I didn't really want to spill who I was meeting with until I knew if she had anything useful to tell me. Even worse than not getting a unique story out of Sydney would be the look on Chase's face if he knew I didn't get a unique story.

But before I could weigh my options, Kyle blurted out, "She's got an exclusive with Sydney Sanders."

I shot him a death look.

"Really?" Chase gave me a quizzical face, one eyebrow raised.

Since the cat was out of the bag, I nodded. "Yeah. I'm meeting her after school."

"But she's grounded."

"I have my ways." I winked at him, doing my best secretive-reporter-type all-knowing smile.

I'm not sure I pulled it off as his other eyebrow headed north.

"You think you can get Sydney to spill how she got the cheats?" Sam asked.

I shrugged. "I dun—" I stopped myself just in time from saying the forbidden word. "I'm going to try," I amended.

"What about Tipkins?" Chase asked.

I gave him a blank look.

"Mr. Tipkins? Your interview today?"

I did a mental face palm. In my excitement over the exclusive with Sydney, I'd totally forgotten about my appointment with Mr. Tipkins. I looked up at the clock on the wall. I had only fifteen minutes before the end of lunch.

"Shoot. I gotta go," I said, shoving a pizza stick in my mouth and grabbing my book bag.

I could have sworn I heard Chase call something like "good luck," behind me as I jogged toward the precalculus room.

Mr. Tipkins was sitting at his desk, a red pen hovering over a stack of papers. He was an older guy with thinning hair that was going gray at the temples. What was left of said hair was slicked back from his forehead in a way that said he stopped paying attention to current fashion decades ago. He had a bushy mustache that matched the salt and pepper up top and twitched intermittently like a nervous tic. His eyes were stuck behind thick glasses, and his clothes looked like they'd come from the Goodwill bargain bins. Brown corduroy pants, black tennis shoes, powder blue, short-sleeved dress shirt. A perpetual smear of ink stained the heel of his right hand from smudging words on the whiteboard.

Even before the cheating bust, Mr. Tipkins had garnered a reputation for being one of the toughest teachers on campus. Sam had taken his summer school precalculus class and swore it took ten years off her life.

"Mr. Tipkins?" I asked, approaching his desk.

He looked up, blinking at me from behind his bifocals. "Yes?"

"Hartley Featherstone?" I said. "From the *Herbert Hoover High Homepage*?"

He nodded. "I know who you are. You're late. I usually leave at lunch."

Due to budget cuts, our school could afford only a set number of full-time teachers who received benefits. The rest had to make do with part-time status, taking only four periods a day.

"Have a seat," he said, indicating a desk in the front row.

I did, pulling out a micro-recorder from my book bag.

"What's that?" Mr. Tipkins asked.

"Recorder. Just so I don't forget any important points."

He frowned. "What's wrong with taking notes? Your hand broken or something?"

"Um. No. I just . . . This is easier."

He narrowed his eyes at me. "Easier. God, technology has made your generation so lazy."

I cleared my throat, not sure I had a response for that. Instead, I put my recorder away and took out a piece of binder paper and a pen.

"Um, I wanted to talk to you about Sydney Sanders."

He nodded. "Another lazy kid."

"You caught Sydney cheating, correct?"

Mr. Tipkins nodded again. "That's right. She thought she was so clever. Can you believe she actually tried to tell me it was just the current fashion to paint letters on your fingernails?"

I grinned, making sure I wrote that quote down. "So, she tried to deny it?"

"'Tried' being the key word," Mr. Tipkins emphasized. "Poor thing's about as sharp as a sphere."

I blinked at him.

"Because a sphere is completely round without any angles or edges?"

I nodded. I knew. It was just the first time I'd heard geometry used in a simile. "So you caught Sydney, and she tried to deny it. At what point did you realize that Quinn was involved as well?"

"About the time we hauled Sydney down to the vice principal's office. When her parents showed up, she said the whole thing had been Quinn's idea."

I raised an eyebrow. Ouch. Giving up your best friend like that was cold. "And did you confront Quinn?"

He nodded. "Sure did. When I told her Sydney gave her up, she was about as discreet as a set of real numbers."

I wasn't sure how discreet numbers could be, let alone fake versus real, but I thought I got the gist. "She confessed?"

He nodded. "She said that it was her idea, but that Sydney had gotten the actual answers and painted both their nails with the letters."

"How did she get the answers?"

Mr. Tipkins threw his hands up. "How should I know?"

"They didn't say?"

He shook his head. "No. They wouldn't tell us how they obtained the answers, so they were both suspended and the administration is looking into it." He leaned in. "Honestly? We'll probably never know."

Not necessarily. In fact, I hoped to answer that very question this afternoon when I talked to Sydney.

"Tell me about the test," I said, switching gears. "How hard would it be for Sydney to steal the answers?"

"Very. I have four different exams for each section we study. I rotate them every four years, so that no student is ever taking a test that anyone else on campus has ever taken. Meaning no upperclassmen can give answers to lowerclassmen. No test ever goes home, even corrected ones. Before the start of every exam, all cell phones are collected to prevent anyone texting answers across the room. I tell you, I spend more time trying to make test answers secure than I do teaching."

I bit my lip. I had to agree he'd devised a pretty good system. "Where are the tests kept?"

"Cabinet." He pointed to a gunmetal gray file cabinet beside the whiteboard. "And I keep it locked whenever I leave the room."

I glanced at the thing. It looked about as old as Mr. Tipkins's cords. I was no expert, but I had a feeling that anyone with a paper clip could break into that thing. Add to that the fact that most classroom doors were left unlocked, and it was hardly Fort Knox in here.

"Are there any other copies?" I asked.

"A master copy is kept in the teachers' lounge, but," he added, wagging a finger at me, "only teachers have access to the lounge. There's no way a student could have slipped in there unnoticed."

This I knew for a fact. Teachers guarded the lounge, their one student-free haven, more heavily than the secret service protected the president. Not only did every teacher need a key to get in, but at any given time of day at least one of them was stationed inside at the coffeepot, standing sentinel over their sacred space. If Sydney had swiped the test, chances were she'd done it in the classroom.

"How would Sydney know which test you were going to give out?"

Again he shrugged. "I told you, I rotate them. I suppose someone could figure out what year we were on by asking around. But it wouldn't be easy."

I nodded. "Just one more question. Are you planning to implement any new anti-cheating measures in light of this incident?"

He nodded vigorously. "You bet I am. From now on, I will inspect everyone's hands before I give them a test. Turning me into a warden more than a teacher," he mumbled. "Are we finished here?"

"Yep. Thanks for your time, Mr. Tipkins," I said, getting up from the desk.

He nodded my way, then pulled a sandwich that looked soggy and limp from a battered paper bag next to his desk.

For a moment, I almost felt sorry for him.

The next two periods dragged so slowly I thought I actually saw the hands of the clock going backward at one point. My mind was completely on my interview with Sydney, only halfway listening as Mrs. Blasberg explained inverse functions and Señorita Gonzalez conjugated verbs. By the time the bell rang, I was practically vibrating with the need to get out. I made a beeline for my locker, quickly shoving my books in and taking homework out. I was just slamming it shut when Ashley Stannic jogged up.

"Hartley, did you read my article online today?" Ashley asked.

"Um, no. Sorry. I'm kinda late—"

"Ohmigod. I got like a total ton of hits! I wrote about Sydney Sanders losing the homecoming nom and who people might write in to fill her place, and everyone was, like, all over it with comments and stuff."

That stopped me in my tracks.

"Wait—Chase told me the Sydney story was mine."

Ashley blinked at me. "Oh. He did? Well, I mean, maybe he changed his mind?"

"Did Chase say you could write about Sydney?"

Ashley nodded. "He edited the article this afternoon during study hall."

I felt anger welling in my stomach. "Where is he now?"

She shrugged, her eyes still wide with innocence. "Um, the workroom, I guess."

I spun around, and marched toward the room. Sydney Sanders wasn't going anywhere. My interview with her could wait. Chase, however, was going to hear an immediate earful.

He had his back to the door when I stormed through it, his head hunched over some piece of paper that Chris Fret was showing him.

"The cheating story is mine!" I announced. Loudly.

So loudly, I think I saw Chris jump. Chase turned around slowly.

"Hartley," he said. His voice was super calm, which of course, just got me more riled up.

"Ashley told me that she got 'a total ton of hits' from her article on Sydney Sanders."

Chase nodded. "Yeah. She did."

"I thought you gave that story to me."

Again Chase nodded slowly. "I'm expecting to print an article from you in tomorrow's edition incorporating the interviews you're getting today. But Ashley had an angle that was interesting, so I let her run with it."

"Just like that? She comes up with something interesting and she's running with my story?"

Chase frowned. "Hey, you come up with something interesting and I'll print that."

I narrowed my eyes. "Are you saying my articles aren't interesting?"

"I'm saying I can't print nothing. You have to give me something worth reading. And the longer you wait, the better the chance someone else is going to beat you to it."

I opened my mouth, shut it, opened it again, realized I didn't have a scathing response, and cursed the way my brain short-circuited at all the wrong times.

"Fine. You'll get your story. And it will be interesting!"

I spun on my heels and slammed the door shut after

me, stalking through the hallways toward the back exit. It took me until I had stomped all the way to the Los Gatos Creek trail before I could finally admit to myself that Chase was right. I didn't have anything interesting. Something I seriously hoped my interview with Sydney would change.

The creek trail snaked behind the football field, down toward a row of condos below. According to Google Earth, Sydney's house was situated just over a mile from the school, the third one down from Vasona Lake on the right.

By the time her back fence came into view, the mid-afternoon sun had created a fine layer of sweat along the back of my neck. I stepped off the trail, carefully setting my backpack down in the grass, and tried to peek over the fence. Tried, because the fence was at least six feet tall and I top out at about 5' 2". Even on tippy-toe, I couldn't see a thing.

"Sydney?" I called, doing something between a stage whisper and an indoor voice.

No one answered.

"It's Hartley?" I called again.

I put my ear to the wooden fence, listening for a reply. Nothing.

I squinted between the slats, but someone had done a crack job of installing this thing. I could only make out the tiniest sliver of the backyard beyond—just enough to see the blue waters of a pool and a pair of deck chairs.

I looked around for something to give me a boost. On the ground was a collection of rocks, but none looked big enough to stand on. On the other side of the trail sat a large oak tree, but I'd given up climbing trees about ten years ago. I called out to Sydney one more time.

"Hey? Sydney? It's me. Hartley."

No answer.

I looked across the trail again. Fine. Tree it was.

I quickly crossed to it, narrowly missing a biker clad in bright yellow spandex. The tree was thick, tall, and definitely sturdy enough to hold all one hundred pounds of me. The only problem was the lowest branch was a good four feet off the ground. I grabbed on to it and pulled my feet up onto the trunk, but they immediately slipped back down, causing my palms to scrape against the branch and depositing me on my butt on the ground.

Ouch.

I picked myself up, trying not to be embarrassed as another biker went by. (Seriously, he was in neon spandex. I wasn't the one who had anything to be embarrassed about.) This time I was able to scramble my legs high enough to lock them around the branch above me. I hung there a moment, like a pig on a spit, before I gathered enough strength to pull my torso up and around to the top side of the branch.

I gave myself a two count to catch my breath, then carefully stuck my foot in the fork of the branches and moved a little bit higher. Once I was high enough that I was starting to get a little dizzy, I scooched out onto a limb that was overhanging the trail.

Sydney's backyard was still a ways away, but from here I could see over the fence. I craned my neck to get my target in view.

What I'd seen through the sliver had been accurate. There was a large pool taking up most of the backyard with a couple of loungers set beside it. I saw a pink beach towel laid out on one, with a glass of iced tea sitting on a table next to it. Signs that someone had been in the yard recently.

I turned my attention to the swimming pool. . . .

And then I saw it.

There, floating in the center of the sparkling blue pool, was Sydney Sanders.

Facedown.

THREE

THE FIRST THING I DID WAS RUN. OKAY, ACTUALLY, THE *FIRST* first thing I did was scream, lose my balance, flail my arms in the air like some kind of uncoordinated bird, then slide down the side of the tree and land on my butt.

Then I ran.

I raced down the pathway as fast as I could, blind panic spurring me on until I reached the bridge where the bike trail connected with the main road and logic started to seep into my brain.

I grabbed my cell and dialed 911, trying my best to keep my voice from shaking out of control as I described what I had seen at Sydney's place. The dispatcher talked to me in annoyingly calm tones (hadn't she heard the dead body part!?) until a police cruiser pulled up to the side of the road and motioned me inside.

I then told my same shaky story to the uniformed officer as he drove me around the block, circling to the front of Teakwood Court, where Sydney's house squatted in the center of the cul-de-sac. It was a one-story, stucco building painted in a gray-blue with bright white trim. A picket fence enclosed the yard, and a couple of orange trees overburdened with fruit flanked the front doors.

Already I could see two more cop cars parked at the curb. A wooden gate sat just to the right of the house, leading to the backyard beyond. Another uniformed officer stood sentinel beside it, arms crossed over his chest, eyes scanning the street for anyone daring to mess up his crime scene.

Which was not a good sign.

During the short wait for the police to arrive and the short ride around the block in the cop car, I'd been trying to convince myself I'd overreacted. I mean, it was possible that Sydney was just playing dead—holding her breath underwater for fun. Maybe she was fine and right now freaking out about the cops intruding on her lazy enjoying-my-suspension-to-the-fullest afternoon.

A big guy with thinning red hair and lots of freckles stepped through the gate from the backyard. He was a little thick around the middle, like he was committed to keeping up the donut-eating-cop stereotype, and wore plain beige khakis and a plaid button-down shirt. Lines creased his face at the corners of his eyes and mouth, which were both currently set in grim lines.

I slumped down in my seat to avoid his gaze. Unfortunately, I knew him all too well.

I'd met Detective Raley when Chase and I had been pursuing that first case together. He'd been in charge of the investigation, and at the time, he'd been the thorn in my side. And, honestly, likely vice versa. But as soon as the killer had been caught, we'd formed a sort of truce. Mostly because we didn't have anything to do with each other anymore.

Until now.

Raley spoke briefly to the cop guarding the back gate, then they both turned toward our police cruiser. Even from across the front lawn, I could see Raley's thick eyebrows lift.

I did a little one finger wave.

Not surprisingly, he didn't wave back.

He mumbled a couple more words to the uniformed cop, gesturing at the yard behind him, then stomped across Mr. Sanders's perfectly mowed lawn toward the police cruiser. I held my breath as he yanked the door open.

"Hartley," he said. Not a question, not a greeting, just a flat monotone statement of fact.

"Detective Raley," I said, trying to kick the shakiness out of my voice and match his non-greeting.

"They tell me you found the body."

I bit my lip. Body. The word choice confirmed that Sydney had not been just lounging in her pool in the unlikely facedown position but was, in fact, dead. A weird range of emotions swam inside my belly. I hadn't been close enough to Sydney to actually call her a friend, but we'd been going to the same high school for two years, so she wasn't really a stranger, either. And as unnerving as finding a stranger dead might have been, finding a girl your own age from your own school that you'd actually DMed with just last night dead hit way too close to home.

"You okay, kid? You look kinda pale."

I gulped down a sudden wave of nausea and nodded. "Uh-huh."

"You're not gonna throw up, are you?"

I shook my head. "Nuh-uhn."

"You sure?" Raley squinted down at me, clearly not convinced.

I did another dry gulp, dragging in a big breath of air with it.

"I think so."

"Good." Raley nodded. "You think you could answer a few questions for me, then?"

I nodded. "I'll try."

"How did you come upon Sydney?"

I did a repeat of the deep-breath thing, then told Raley

that I'd been "strolling" along the bike trail on my way home from school when I'd seen Sydney in the pool, freaked, ran, and called 911.

"Wait—" Raley said, putting up a hand, "you were on your way home from school?"

I nodded.

"But you live that way," he said, pointing in the opposite direction from the trail.

"It was a nice day. I thought I'd take a little detour."

Raley stared down at me, leaning in so close I could see right up his nose. I tried not to stare, lest that nausea come back.

"A detour?"

"Yep. I'm . . . a nature lover."

Yeah, I know. That sounded lame even to my own ears. But I wasn't sure just yet how much I wanted to share with Raley. He had a habit of interpreting situations his own way, and I figured that me planning to meet a dead girl and spying on her from a tree was not a situation he would interpret in a positive way.

"How did you see Sydney?" Raley asked.

"What do you mean?"

"I mean the back fence is six feet high. How did you manage to see in the yard?"

"Through a crack in the fence?"

"Is that a question?"

I cleared my throat. "No."

Raley gave me a stare down again, but, thankfully, let it go.

"How well did you know Sydney?" he asked instead.

I shrugged. "Not that well. We go to the same school."

"Was she there today?"

I shook my head. "No. She's suspended. She cheated on a test."

Raley raised an eyebrow. "Suspended. I guess she was pretty upset about that?"

"I guess. Like I said, we weren't really that close." I paused. "Why?"

Raley avoided my eyes. "No reason. Just asking."

Huh.

"How had Sydney seemed before she was suspended?"

I narrowed my eyes. "'Seemed?'"

He shrugged. "Was she generally a happy person, or did she keep to herself?"

"She was in the running for homecoming queen until two days ago."

He leaned in. "She lost?"

"She was kicked off the court when she got caught cheating."

He raised an eyebrow. "Suspended and kicked off the homecoming court. So, I'd guess she was upset."

I narrowed my eyes at him again, trying to follow his

train of thought. "Why does it matter if Sydney was upset? This was an accident."

Raley looked at me, his face a blank, unreadable cop thing.

"It *was* an accident, right?" I repeated.

He sighed. "It's too soon to tell. At this point we need to explore all possibilities."

"Meaning . . . ?"

"Meaning most teenage deaths that we investigate end up being self-inflicted."

I blinked at him. "Suicide?"

Raley nodded.

"Oh no. You've got this all wrong." I shook my head violently from side to side. "No, that doesn't make any sense. Sydney wasn't suicidal."

"I thought you said you didn't know her well," Raley countered.

"Not that well, but trust me, Sydney did not commit suicide."

"You just said she was suspended for cheating. Maybe the guilt overwhelmed her?"

I let out a laugh, then quickly stifled it as Raley shot me a look.

"Look, Sydney wasn't the guilty type," I explained. "For example, Erin Carter was the front-runner for homecoming queen. Until Sydney started a rumor that

Erin had lice. Suddenly no one would come within five feet of Erin, and the school nurse even came in to check her head right in the middle of PE. Trust me, guilt was not in Sydney's repertoire."

Raley did the deep-sigh thing again, and I looked away to avoid seeing his nose hairs vibrate with the effort. "Look, it's too early to tell much of anything at this point. All I can say is that it doesn't look like an accident."

"What do you mean? She drowned, right? That can happen, can't it?"

"We have to wait for the ME's report, but it doesn't look like she drowned. We found something in the pool with her."

"Something?"

"Her laptop."

"What do you mean?" I asked, trying to process the information.

"It was plugged into an outdoor wall outlet. Our best guess is that Sydney jumped into the pool with her laptop and electrocuted herself."

I blinked at him, letting this sink in. He had a point. That hardly seemed like an accident. Even if Sydney had been online poolside, what were the chances she'd decide to take a dip with her computer? No one was that stupid, not even Sydney Sanders.

On the other hand, I was having a hard time wrapping

my brain around the idea of Sydney ending her life. Sure, she'd been tweeting some pretty unhappy stuff lately, but there was a huge gulf between saying your life sucked and actually ending it. And if you were going to end it, wouldn't you want to wait until after you had unburdened yourself to the reporter you were supposed to meet?

"That just doesn't make any sense. I mean, why would she kill herself before she—"

I stopped myself just in time.

Raley leaned in, his bushy eyebrows moving north. "Before she what?"

I shut my mouth with a click.

"Before . . . the homecoming dance," I finished lamely.

That seemed to satisfy Raley as he just shrugged. "It's hard to say what goes through a suicidal person's mind."

I bit my lip. I was pretty sure this person wasn't suicidal. Which left only one alternative.

Sydney Sanders's death was a homicide.

"It was a homicide," I told Sam two hours later as I sat cross-legged on my bed.

"No fluffin' way!"

I paused. "Wait—'fluffin''?"

Sam shrugged. "I was getting tired of 'effing.' It was too obvious, you know? I'm experimenting with some alternatives."

"Well, fluffin' is . . . creative." I shook my head. "But, more important, yes way, Sydney was totally murdered."

As soon as I'd arrived home in a police cruiser, Mom had jumped into total SMother mode, wigging out that I was with the police (again), hugging me to within an inch of my life when she heard the cop say one of my classmates had been killed (which, honestly, was a little comforting), then totally freaking that I'd been the one to find a dead body. (Again. Which, I had to admit, was totally freaky.) She'd immediately gone into the kitchen and made her version of comfort food, while I'd immediately called Sam and told her she had to come over ASAP. Both Sam and the rice cakes with flaxseed butter had arrived at the same time, and I'd used the comfort fuel to spill the whole story.

"So," Sam said, grabbing a rice cake. She held it up to her nose, sniffed, then thought better of it, and placed it back on the plate. "Raley told you Sydney was murdered?"

"Well, not exactly," I hedged. "He thinks she committed suicide."

While I'd expected Sam to have the same shocked reaction I'd had at the idea, she just slowly nodded. "I can see that."

I stared at her. "You're kidding, right? I mean, we're talking about a girl who incorporated cheats into her nail-polish design. She was scheming. Underhanded. Remorseless. Not the type to give it all up."

"But she was depressed," Sam pointed out. "She tweeted four times this afternoon alone talking about how miserable she was."

"You follow Sydney on Twitter?" I asked.

Sam nodded. "She was captain of the lacrosse team. We all followed her."

"What did she say?" I asked as Sam pulled out her phone. I leaned in to read the screen over her shoulder.

"Well, the first one was about how it sucks that her homecoming dress is going to waste. The second was about how it sucks that no one is around to call until lunch. One was about how it sucks that we can't sunbathe anymore 'cause of sucky skin cancer,'" she said, scrolling through the tweets. "And the last one was about how much it sucks being alone by the pool on a sunny beautiful day."

"That last one," I said, stabbing a finger at her phone. "When did she write that?"

"Um . . ." Sam squinted at the readout. "Three-oh-five."

I felt a sudden chill run up my spine. "I was outside her place just a couple minutes later. She must have sent that tweet right before . . ."

Sam's eyes got all big and round. "She went in the pool," she finished for me. "Ohmigod. She was killed while tweeting. It was Twittercide!"

Again that too-close-for-comfort ball of nausea flared

up in my stomach. I grabbed a rice cake, chewing quickly to wash down the sensation.

"Honestly, I think that's one more point against Sydney having killed herself," I decided. "If she was tweeting when she died, wouldn't she have left some sort of message? Tweeted why she was doing it? A 'good-bye cruel world' kind of thing?"

Sam nodded. "Totally. That would have been classic Sydney." She paused. "But why would anyone want to kill her?"

"I can think of one reason," I answered. "She was about to talk to me. Maybe whatever she was going to tell me was something that someone didn't want to get out."

Sam's eyes went big again. "Whoa. You killed Sydney!"

I shifted uncomfortably on my patchwork comforter. "No I didn't! I mean, not exactly. But the point is that the cops all think it was suicide, and we're the only ones who know it was actually homicide."

"Meaning?"

I bit my lip. "Meaning," I said, the realization sinking in, "it's up to us to figure out who really killed Sydney."

Which, I realized the next morning, was easier said than done. As I'd mentioned to Raley, you didn't get to be the homecoming queen front-runner by being a wallflower. Sydney had been visible, active in everything at school, and not afraid to do whatever she needed to in order to get ahead. Needless to say, Sydney had as many enemies as she did friends. However, there was one person who would qualify at the moment as both Sydney's best friend and worst enemy: Quinn Leslie, the former BFF who Sydney had ratted out to the principal when she'd been caught cheating.

Unfortunately, Quinn had been suspended along with Sydney, so cornering her during school was not an option. Instead, I made plans to visit her during lunch, and impatiently sat through first period, where I got no less than six texts asking if it was true that I'd found a dead body. Again. During second, I got two gleeful tweets announcing that Sydney's suicide meant Mrs. Perry was delaying the chem midterm. During third, two texts said black armbands would be available in the quad at lunch. And during fourth, I got a tweet with a link to the official Sydney Sanders memorial page on Facebook, already outfitted with PayPal links to donate to teen-suicide prevention programs.

By lunch period, everyone on campus was buzzing about the suicide that I was sure was not a suicide, and I was more anxious than ever to prove just that. I was shoving books into my locker and planning my strategy for confronting Quinn when Chase cornered me.

"Hey, Hart," he said. "Where are we on Sydney's story?"

"I'm fine, thanks for asking. Finding her dead body

didn't rattle me at all," I said, heavy on the sarcasm.

Chase grinned. "Okay, my bad. How are you Hartley? Holding up?"

"Yes."

"Good. So, where are we on the story?"

I rolled my eyes. "We're good. Fine. Great."

"Meaning?"

"Meaning, I'm working a *unique* angle," I said, emphasizing the word.

Again he grinned at me. "Lay it on me, Featherstone."

And, considering he was my editor, I did, outlining how I thought someone had committed, as Sam had put it, "Twittercide." When I was finished, Chase's eyebrows were drawn together in a frown.

"But I thought the police were looking at her death as a suicide?"

I nodded. "They are. But they're wrong."

"And why do you think that?"

"Because of the meeting Sydney had set up with me for yesterday afternoon. She knew I was working on the story, and she was going to tell me something."

"What?"

"I dunno."

Chase shot me a look. But before he could comment, I quickly backtracked, "I mean, she died before she could tell me."

"Who knew you were going to talk to her?"

I shrugged. "You, Sam, Kyle. Anyone that Sydney might have told."

"Which doesn't narrow things down much."

"No, but if she was suicidal, wouldn't she wait until after she'd told me whatever it was she wanted to get off her chest?"

Chase looked at me for a long moment. "How do you know she wasn't going to tell you to back off and leave her alone? Maybe she felt so persecuted and hounded by the entire school—you included—that she killed herself."

I bit my lip. "Please don't say she killed herself because of me."

"I didn't. I just think that if we're going to run with a story saying she definitely didn't kill herself, we need to offer more than circumstantial evidence. We need proof."

I nodded. "Right. That's what I intend to get."

"How?"

"Quinn Leslie."

"The girl Sydney got caught cheating with?"

I nodded. "And her former best friend. If anyone had a reason to hate Sydney, it would be her."

Chase stared at me as he chewed on this angle. "When are you going to talk to her?"

"I'd planned on now."

"Cool. I'll go with you."

I paused. "I can do this on my own. I'm not gonna screw up," I said, unable to help the defensive edge that crept into my voice.

Chase grinned, showing off one dimple in his left cheek. "I know. But I'm in the mood for a little entertainment."

I opened my mouth to respond, but he didn't wait. Instead, he slammed my locker shut for me and turned toward the back parking lot.

"You coming, Featherstone?" he said over his shoulder.

While I wasn't thrilled with being considered "entertainment," I had little choice but to follow.

I only hoped Quinn didn't mind a crowd.

FOUR

UNFORTUNATELY, QUINN LIVED A GOOD FIVE MILES AWAY from the school, which left me with two choices to get to her before sixth period started: the city bus or Chase's car.

As soon as I'd turned sixteen, Mom had started the lectures about riding in cars with my friends who had their licenses: (1) never ride with more than three people at a time, (2) do not turn on the radio, as it distracts the driver, and (3) do not get in any vehicle that doesn't look like it's passed a ten-point safety inspection in the last six months. Chase's car was a 1985 Camaro with a dented back bumper, a muffler that was holding on for dear life, and a crack down the right side of the windshield. It wouldn't pass a two-point safety inspection. But more disturbing than that car was Chase's driving itself. On the scant few occasions where I'd ridden with him, I'd felt like I was in the running for a NASCAR cup.

He unlocked the passenger-side door of the Camaro and held it open for me.

I stared at it.

"You getting in or what?" he asked.

I bit my lip.

"Earth to Hartley?"

"I'm thinking."

Chase rolled his eyes. "Just get in the car, Hart."

He walked around to the driver's side, got in, and gunned the engine, creating a cloud of black smoke in the region of his muffler (which I was 99 percent sure was just for show).

Without much other choice, I hopped in, buckled my seat belt, and gripped the side door for dear life.

The first thing Chase did was crank up the radio so high the Camaro's windows vibrated.

I said a silent prayer and held on tight.

Ten minutes, two "orange" lights, and three "California stops" later, we arrived in front of the two-story ranch house listed under Quinn's name in our school's buzz book.

I pried my fingers out of the white-knuckled position they'd frozen into, then silently counted to see if my teeth were still intact. Yep, all there, despite rattling together like Tic Tacs as we'd caught air on the speed bumps leading to her neighborhood.

Chase, oblivious to my concerns, hopped out of the car, shoving his hands in his pockets as we made our way up the front walk. He rang the bell, and a beat later, it was opened by a guy with dark hair, dark eyes, and a dark-looking scowl on his face.

"Yeah?" he asked.

I shifted from foot to foot, suddenly nervous. "Um, hi," I said, doing a little wave. "Is Quinn here?"

"Quinn's grounded," he said, moving to shut the door.

"Wait!" I said, raising a hand.

He paused, lifted an eyebrow at me, but continued the scowl thing.

"We're, uh . . . here about homework," I lied.

Chase shot me a look but thankfully remained silent.

"Homework?" the guy asked.

"Um, yeah. Quinn's teachers didn't want her to get behind so we're here to tell her what her homework is."

He paused a moment, then looked from me to Chase. Then back at me. Clearly Chase wasn't what he'd expect in a messenger of the teachers, but he finally shrugged. "Fine," he said. "I'll get her. But she has five minutes, that's it."

I nodded. Hopefully that was all we needed.

He stepped back, pulling the door shut again, as we heard him call out to Quinn.

Chase elbowed me in the ribs. "Nice one, Featherstone," he whispered.

I tried not to grin at the praise as the door opened again to reveal Quinn.

While Quinn and Sydney had been best friends all through high school, the two could not be more opposite in the looks department. Sydney had been brunette, green eyed, tall. She had long, straight hair that was usually worn in a ponytail or stylish-sloppy bun, and had her finger (and closet) firmly on the pulse of the latest fashions. Not only had Sydney been captain of the lacrosse team, a starting pitcher on the girls' softball team, and a 100-meter-dash record holder on the track team, she was also on the debate team, the yearbook club, and was head of the Spirit Week committee.

Quinn's extracurricular activities, on the other hand, started and ended with the athletics department. She was a sporty girl through and through. The only time she wasn't wearing a pair of sweats was when she was in an HHH jersey of some sort. Quinn was slimmer than Sydney had been—all lean muscle—and half Japanese, giving her pale skin, straight dark hair, and brown almond-shaped eyes that created an exotic look.

Today, Quinn was wearing the Sporty Girl uniform of pink sweatpants, a T-shirt, and Ugg boots. The word *Juicy* was written down the right leg of her sweats, which was ironic, considering I couldn't see an ounce of body fat on her.

While Sydney may have been her *ex*-BFF, I could see that Quinn's eyes were red-rimmed and puffy, like she'd spent a fair amount of the morning crying. I suddenly felt bad for her and just a little guilty that we were there to question her as a suspect.

"Hey, Quinn," I said as she stared at the two of us on her doorstep. "I'm Hartley. I'm on the *Herbert Hoover High Homepage*."

Quinn nodded, her ponytail bobbing up and down behind her. "I recognize you," she said.

"We wanted to ask you some questions about Sydney for the paper," Chase added.

"Oh." Quinn's eyes hit the ground. "Um, sure, I guess."

"You two were friends, right?" Chase asked.

Quinn nodded, her eyes flickering up from the cement porch. "Yeah. Since sixth grade."

"But she's the reason you're suspended?" I asked.

For just a second I could have sworn I saw anger flash through her veil of grief, but it was quickly swallowed up as Quinn replied. "Yeah, but she was my best friend for four years. We did everything together, you know?"

"Including cheat on tests," Chase pointed out.

Quinn bit her lip. "Look, it was stupid. I know."

"Sydney told the principal that it was your idea."

"It was. And it was stupid," Quinn repeated.

"Then why did you do it?" I asked.

"Because I needed to get a good grade on that test! Look, Mr. Tipkins is one of the hardest teachers on campus. I'm not a brainy kind of person, you know? I mean, math isn't my thing. I was struggling just to get a C in that class, and unless I got a three-point-four overall GPA, I was going to get cut from the lacrosse team."

"Lacrosse means that much to you?" I asked. According to Sam, it was just this side of hell on earth. Then again the only thing sporty about Sam was her collection of cute hoodies.

"I need to stay on the team," Quinn explained. "I'm counting on a sports scholarship. My parents can barely afford my brother going to community college. There's no way they can foot the bill for a UC."

I nodded. I couldn't count how many thinly (and sometimes not so thinly) veiled references to the cost of college my own mom made on a daily basis. The day I started looking at UC Berkeley, she'd started playing the lottery.

"Why did Sydney cheat?" Chase asked. "Was math not her thing, either?"

Quinn paused. "Actually, Sydney was pretty good at math. But lately, with lacrosse and homecoming plus her after-school stuff, she didn't have any time to study. When

I suggested cheating, she was relieved. Like she had one less thing to worry about."

"Did she seem overly worried to you?" Chase asked, jumping on the word. "Stressed, depressed . . . suicidal?"

Quinn pursed her lips together, taking a moment with that one. "If you had asked me that last week, I would have said no way. Sydney was all about overachieving. And overachievers don't throw in the towel. But now . . ." She shrugged her shoulders in indecision. "Honestly, I don't know. I mean, I hadn't really seen her much since Tuesday."

"You mean, since she ratted you out?" Chase said, coming to the point of our interrogation.

Quinn turned on him, that flash of anger clearly visible this time. "Yeah. She did."

"Which must have pissed you off," I added.

Quinn nodded. "Yeah, it did. It was her idea to put the answers on our nails. I told her we should just memorize them, but she said she didn't have time. Then she gets caught, just like I said she would, and she points a finger at me? Totally unfair."

"I agree," I said. "So unfair. Where were you yesterday after school?"

Quinn cocked her head to the side. "What do you mean?"

"I mean, do you have an alibi for Sydney's time of death?"

She blinked her dark eyes at me. Then she turned to Chase. "Is she for real?"

"Unfortunately," Chase mumbled. Though, I could have sworn I saw the corner of his mouth tilt upward into a grin.

"Look, if Sydney wasn't suicidal, she must have been killed by someone else," I jumped in. "You seem to have a pretty good motive."

Quinn shook her head from side to side so hard her ponytail swished in the breeze behind her. "No way. Look, yes, I was pissed at Sydney, but I'm not a killer!"

"Then where were you?" I asked again.

"Here! Geez, I'm grounded for the rest of my natural life. I can't even sneeze without my dad hovering over me," she said, gesturing behind herself. "Like I could get out to kill someone."

She had a good point. Dad seemed pretty vigilant. I felt my best-friend-killer theory slowly crumbling.

"Do you know anyone else who might have had a problem with Sydney?" I asked instead.

Quinn shrugged again. "No clue. I mean, we totally creamed West San Jose High last week at the game."

"How did you and Sydney get the answers in the first place?" Chase pressed, switching gears.

Quinn paused, looking from him to me. "Sydney bought them."

I raised an eyebrow. "From who?"

She gave me a blank look. "Got me."

I shot her a "get real" look.

"Seriously!" she protested. "I don't know where Sydney got them. I told her, 'Wouldn't it be cool if we could just get the answers to the test?' and the next thing I know, Sydney says she's got someone willing to sell them to her."

"And she didn't tell you who it was?"

Quinn shook her head. "She didn't know, either. The buy was all set up anonymously."

"How?" I asked.

"Some senior gave her this cell number. She texted the guy which class she wanted the answers for, then exchanged cash for them."

"Where did she do the exchange?" I asked.

"At the football game last Friday night. That's where this guy does business. She was supposed to put the money under a big rock outside the mascot's dressing room before the game started. Then she went back at halftime, and the answers were waiting for her there."

I nodded. It sounded like a perfect drop place to me. Lots of people would be around at the game, so it wasn't likely the guy selling cheats would stand out. But the mascot room was isolated enough that it was a safe bet no one else would stumble across the cash before he could.

"He does this every Friday?" Chase asked.

Quinn nodded. "That's what Sydney said."

"Quinn," her dad called from inside the house. Apparently our five minutes was up.

"I gotta go," she said. She moved to close the door but paused just before she got there. "Look, I would never hurt Sydney. We had our differences, but she was my best friend. I don't know what I'm gonna do without her."

"So," Chase said as we walked back down the front walk to his car. "Do we believe her?"

I shrugged. "She could have slipped away from her dad long enough to shove Sydney into the swimming pool."

Chase nodded. "It's possible." He opened the Camaro's driver-side door (which groaned loudly in protest) and got in. "But I say we follow the cheating angle."

I followed suit, steeling myself for another wild ride back to school. "So you think Quinn was telling the truth about how they got the answers?"

Chase shrugged. "Well, there's only one way to find out." He turned to me, grinned, then shot me a wink as he gunned the engine. "Want to go to the football game with me tonight, Featherstone?"

FIVE

IT WASN'T UNTIL LAST PERIOD WAS OVER THAT I GOT A chance to fill Sam in on what Quinn had said. She was on the west field again, at lacrosse practice. Only today, I noticed as I made my way toward the bleachers, the team had a whole different vibe. While Sydney and Quinn being suspended might have dampened their hopes of making nationals this year, Sydney's death had put a virtual black cloud over the team, seeming to cause the girls to run just a little slower, the coach to yell just a little softer, and the energy level to fall several enthusiasm notches down the spirit scale. On the upside, Sam was only two yards behind all the other players today instead of three.

I waited until the coach blew her whistle, signaling a water break, before hailing Sam over.

"Hey," she said, panting as she jogged toward me. "I

think I'm getting the hang of this." She leaned on her stick, taking in deep breaths. "I almost touched the ball once today."

"Awesome!" I had to hand it to her—she was optimistic if nothing else. Quickly I filled her in on Chase's and my interview with Quinn.

"So do you think she did it?" Sam asked when I was finished.

I shook my head. "Not sure. Her alibi seems solid enough, but I still like her on motive. Being ratted out to the vice P is a pretty big thing to forgive."

Sam nodded. "True."

"But," I hedged, "Chase has a point about the test answers. It's just as likely Sydney knew something about who was selling them and the guy killed her to avoid exposure."

"So you're going to the football game tonight to find him?"

I nodded, then replayed the plan Chase and I had concocted in the car as we'd driven back from Quinn's house. It was pretty simple, really. We'd wait until the game started, then hide out where we could watch the mascot room. As soon as the cheat seller showed up to collect his cash and drop off that week's answers, we'd catch him.

"Wait," Sam said when I'd finished. "You and Chase are going?"

"Yeah."

"As in together?"

"Well, kinda . . ."

"As in you're going to the football game together?"

"I'm not really sure if—"

"Ohmigod. Did Chase ask you out?"

"No!" I made a "pft" sound through my teeth. "God no. We're going to the game to catch the cheater. It's a stakeout. That's it."

"But he did ask you to go with him, right?"

I pursed my lips together, trying to remember what he'd said. "Well, yeah. But I'm sure he didn't mean *with him* with him."

"Tell me the exact words he used," Sam ordered, leaning forward on her stick.

"He said, 'Want to go to the football game with me?'"

Sam threw her hands up. "That's it. He asked you out. On a date."

I shook my head. "I really don't think he meant it like that."

"Are you sure?" Sam narrowed her eyes at me.

"Yes. No. I . . . I don't know! He said it, and he winked at me."

"Whoa!" Sam dropped her stick, putting both hands up. "You didn't mention a wink. You never said anything about a wink!"

"Why? What's the wink mean?" I asked, starting to get a little nervous.

"Ohmigod, Hartley. He totally fluffin' asked you out."

"No." I shook my head. "Absolutely not." I paused. "I mean, I don't think he did."

"As soon as practice is over, we're getting you home and dressed to kill just in case."

I rolled my eyes. "This is so not like that, Sam."

"Yeah, well, better safe than sorry."

An hour later, the entire contents of my closet were strewn out on my bed, and I was beginning to feel sorry I'd ever agreed to let Sam help me play it safe.

She held up a pair of jeans and a tank top with a sparkly butterfly on the front.

"The jeans say casual, but the top says flirty."

"I'm not sure about flirty—" I started, but Sam ran right over me. She was in her element, in the zone.

And I was in serious trouble.

"But see, this skirt," she said, holding up a white denim mini, "says flirty, and if you pair it with this pink Henley," she added, holding up the button-top shirt, "it says casual, yet feminine, too."

"I like casual," I said, hanging on that word.

"On the other hand," Sam said, dropping the outfit in a heap on my floor as she grabbed another pair of hangers.

"This tube dress totally says sophisticated, and if you pair it with this denim jacket and cowboy boots, it says chic with an edge."

I rolled my eyes. My clothes were going to be doing a lot of talking tonight.

"Sam, the game starts in half an hour. Can we please just pick something?"

Her eyes ping-ponged between the casual-flirty and the flirty-casual outfits before she finally shoved the tube dress at me. "We're going edgy chic. And I think I can glam your makeup just enough to pull this off."

"Wait—makeup?" I wore a little mascara on a daily basis and had a tube of pink lip gloss conveniently tucked in my book bag, but that was about it.

Sam must have read my mind as she waved me off. "Don't worry. I have an emergency touch-up kit in my backpack. We'll have you looking date ready in no time."

Somehow that did little to relieve my worry.

Worry that was well-founded as, by the time Sam was done with me, I was casual-chic-flirty, my makeup was edgy-sophisticated-glam, and my nerves were stretched-to-their-limit raw.

Not to mention that my heels (I'd drawn the line at cowboy boots) were Mom-will-never-approve high.

I slowly walked downstairs, Sam a step behind me. Mom was at the kitchen table, directly in the line of sight of the front door. She had her laptop out again, her eyes intent on the screen as she scrolled with her right hand.

"Too tall," she muttered to herself. Some more scrolling. "Too skinny." Scrolling again. Then Mom made a disgusted face. "Uh, too . . . hairy."

Mental face palm. Mom was on Match again.

I took a tentative step forward.

She didn't look up.

I tiptoed down the rest of the stairs, one eye on Mom, one eye on the door.

If she heard me, she didn't register it.

Two feet from the front door, I took a deep breath and made a break for it.

"ByeMomgoingtothefootballgameseeyalater," I quickly said as I thrust the front door open.

"Have fun," she called. Her gaze never left the computer screen.

I had a bad feeling a Match intervention was going to be needed at some point.

Herbert Hoover High home games are total community events. Our school is set smack in the middle of San Jose, one of the largest cities in California and quickly filling with enough people to rival both Los Angeles and San Diego in population. Which means that San Jose tends to divide itself into smaller communities within the larger city, each section retaining its own small-town feel: Willow Glen in the north, Cambrian just south of that, Almaden Valley farther south, and our little section, Blossom Grove, nestled up against the Santa Cruz Mountains—where Friday nights you were either tucked in at home watching a Netflix or at the football game.

Honestly, most of the time I was more of a Netflix girl. School was a place I spent six hours a day, five days a week, usually under duress. I wasn't really that into spending extra time there. But, I realized as I navigated the sea of people crowding the parking lot pre-game, I was in the minority.

Guys in HHH Windbreakers and girls in hoodies and Uggs gathered in groups, giggling, yelling, hailing friends, all converging on the stadium, which was lit up like daylight against the growing dusk outside. Just beyond the entrance gate were hot dog and nacho carts, a long line trailing behind them that spanned the length of the fence. The smell was intoxicating, reminding me that in Sam's flurry of clothes, I hadn't taken time to eat dinner. I could hear cheers from inside the stadium signaling that cheerleaders were on the field throwing their high kicks and oozing school spirit. The game that night was against Saratoga High, a longtime rival of HHH, which meant the administration was on high prank alert and the student body was on high party alert.

"Hartley?" I heard someone call my name. "Over here."

I looked up to see Chase hailing me from the other side of the nacho cart. He was in the same clothes he'd worn to school earlier—jeans and black boots, though he'd covered up his T-shirt with a black hoodie that had a surfer on the front. He already had a cardboard container of nachos in his hands, steam rising from the gooey cheese. I quickly jogged over to him.

"Hey. Sorry I'm late. I had to walk," I said by way of greeting.

He paused, then cocked his head at me. "You look different."

Immediately I felt myself blushing. "Nope, I'm the same."

Chase shook his head. "No. Something's different." He squinted through the dusk. "Are you wearing eye shadow?"

"No!" I ducked my head again, this time rubbing at my upper lids to get some of the gunk off. "I'm just . . . it's the lighting. It's dark out here."

Chase grinned. "Well, I like it. You look good in the dark."

My cheeks heated even further, and I wasn't even sure if that was a compliment or not. "Thanks," I mumbled, then grabbed a nacho and shoved it into my mouth to cover my embarrassment.

Chase grinned even wider. "Gee, help yourself."

I did, grabbing another nacho and totally ignoring his sarcasm.

"The game's about to start," Chase said, nodding toward the stadium, where the cheers were rising to an emotional high. "We should get in place before the cheat guy shows up."

I nodded, grabbing one more nacho before following him around the back out of the stadium and to the right, where a line of portable classrooms sat.

While every politician that ever runs for office in California uses improving schools as a platform, the truth is that our schools are perpetually broke. Meaning that classrooms are busting at the seams, and the overflow is usually housed in portable units parked in rows on any available space of land near the school. Though the word *portable* is a bit of a lie because they never actually move. In fact, my mom took geometry class in the very same "temporary" portable that I had it in with Mrs. Britton sophomore year.

The row of portables outside the stadium housed the extracurricular programs that lacked funding for real classrooms, including the pottery room, the shared room for glee club and choir, and the room that housed the extra football uniforms and the mascot's costume.

It wasn't at every school that mascots got their own

changing rooms, but in our case he did. Mostly because our mascot was the Herbert Hoover High donkey, who everyone in the area fondly referred to as the HHH jackass. Last year, our football team thought it would be fun to sneak into the jackass's locker and switch out the contents of his water bottle for vodka right before the last home game. And it might actually have been funny if the guy in the jackass suit hadn't downed the beverage and vomited all over the field. Then, in a drunken stupor that left the administration red-faced and the fans cheering harder than on any other night of the year, he'd ended up braying at the cheerleaders and knocking the tuba player in the marching band over on his butt.

After that, the HHH donkey always changed in his own room.

Outside of which was a towering palm tree with a large gray rock sitting at its base.

I elbowed Chase in the ribs and pointed. "That must be where he does the drop."

Chase nodded, then quickly looked around. To our right was the choir portable, to the left a line of bushes separating us from the condo complex next door. "We'll hide behind the bushes," he decreed.

Before I could protest that my heels weren't all that practical for stomping through foliage, he'd already slipped between two hedges and disappeared.

Fab. Left with little choice, I followed, ducking as the brush grabbed at my hair, leaving little wet deposits on my denim jacket. Behind the bush, I found Chase squatting in the dirt. I bent my knees, lowering myself beside him while trying not to let my tube dress ride too far up my thighs.

Chase glanced over. "Nice dress," he whispered, his gaze lingering on the rising hem just a little too long.

I tugged it down over my knees, stretching it in a way that I'm sure would have had Sam cringing. "Thanks," I mumbled.

We sat in silence a few more minutes, crouching in the dirt. I felt my feet starting to fall asleep as the strap of my heels cut into my ankles.

Then Chase leaned in close. "Hey."

"What?" I whispered back.

"Are you wearing perfume?"

I swallowed hard. "No," I lied. "Why would I be wearing perfume?"

Chase shrugged. "Maybe you're going out later?"

I gritted my teeth together. Sam was so going to hear about this.

Chase sniffed the air. "You sure you're not wearing anything? It smells like jasmine."

"Must be the bushes," I said.

Chase shifted. "I don't think there are any jasmine bushes around here. Don't they have flowers?"

"I don't think so."

"Yeah, little white ones, right? There are definitely no little white flowers on these bushes."

"Shhh!" I said. "Someone's coming."

Which, thankfully, was true.

Through the shadows, I saw a guy walking toward the mascot room, head down, hands in pockets, the hood of his sweatshirt pulled up, obscuring his face. Nothing about his clothes stood out as distinguishable from any of the other hundreds of students at the game tonight.

"He's early," Chase whispered. "It's not halftime yet."

"Maybe he needs the cash now. Maybe he wants nachos," I guessed, feeling my own stomach growl.

Chase and I watched as the figure paused outside the mascot room. He looked over both shoulders, then quickly leaned down in front of the rock by the palm tree.

"He's picking up the cash!" I whispered. "Let's go!"

Chase popped up from the ground, crashing through the bushes toward the figure. I followed a step behind, feeling my heels sink into the dirt as I tried not to step on anything too squishy or gross. Mud spattered up onto my legs as I emerged from the brush, tripping over a root on the ground.

Just in time to see the guy straighten up, turn away, and shove his hands back in his pockets.

"Hey!" Chase yelled. "Don't move!"

Which, of course, the guy totally ignored. Instead, he spun around, took one look at Chase barreling down on him, and bolted, taking off in the direction of the choir portable at a dead run.

Chase didn't miss a beat, running after the guy as he rounded the corner of the classroom.

I tottered after them as fast as I could, but actual running in three-inch heels and a tube dress was a total joke.

I came to the edge of the classroom and saw Chase still running after the guy. The other guy had a head start, but Chase was taller and easily gained on him. By the time they made it to the end of the line of portables, Chase was almost on top of him. I watched as he leaped forward, tackling the other guy from behind and bringing him crashing to the ground with a grunt.

I clacked forward on the blacktop with my heels, closing in on the pair as Chase flipped the guy over onto his back. It was dark back here, but the ambient glow from the stadium provided just enough light to make out his features as I got my first good look at the guy's face. And realized it was one I knew well.

Chris Fret, the *HHH Homepage*'s sportswriter.

SIX

"NO FLUFFIN' WAY!" I YELLED, DISBELIEF HITTING ME AS I finally caught up to the pair.

I'd known Chris since fifth grade, lived just two blocks away from him, and had spent every other afternoon with him at the paper for the last two months. While he was on the skinny side to actually play football, he knew the sport inside and out, and attended every single game for the paper. His commentary was smart, funny, and thorough, making it entertaining reading even for those of us who weren't obsessed with stats and scores. Chris was a decent student, a nice guy, and an asset to the paper.

And the last person I would have expected to be selling cheats to the student body.

Chris blinked, his gaze going from Chase to me. "Guys?" he asked, confusion lacing his voice. "Dude, what's goin' on?"

"I should ask you the same thing," Chase growled.

"Chris, how could you?" I asked, realizing I sounded frighteningly like my mom when she'd clucked her disappointed tongue at my less than stellar report card last semester.

"What?" he said, his eyes still bouncing back and forth. "How could I what?"

"Drop the act, Chris," Chase told him. "We caught you selling them red-handed."

"Dude, 'selling'? What are you talking about?"

"You were picking up the payment," I said.

Chris blinked. "I swear I wasn't picking up anything."

Chase gave him a hard stare then hauled him to his feet by his armpits. "You'd better start telling the truth or else . . ." he said, letting the rest of that threat hang in the air.

Chris made a small yipping sound in Chase's grip. "Wait, you've got this all wrong. I'm innocent, I promise."

"Then what the hell were you just doing?" Chase asked, his right hand still fisted in Chris's shirt.

Chris licked his lips. "Okay, fine. Look, I was leaving payment under the rock."

"Leaving payment?"

Chris nodded. "For the answers to Mrs. Perry's chem quiz on Monday."

Mental face palm. Chris wasn't selling the cheats; he was buying them.

"The money was supposed to be under the rock before

the game started, and the text said the answers would be there by halftime."

"But the game's already started," I pointed out.

Chris shrugged sheepishly. "I'm a little late. I had to convince my dad to let me borrow the car first."

I narrowed my eyes at him, and Chase leaned in with a growl. Chris yipped again.

"I'm telling the truth!"

"What are you doing buying answers, Chris?" Chase asked. "You want to get suspended, too?"

Chris's cheeks tinged pink with guilt. "Look, you can't tell anyone, okay? My dad threatened to take away my driving privileges if I didn't keep my grades up. I'm totally failing chem, and if I don't pass this quiz, I can say adios to my dad's station wagon."

"Ever heard of studying?" Chase asked.

Chris blinked at him. "Between being at all the games, and the paper, and my after-school job, I don't have time to study!"

I rolled my eyes.

"Okay, then tell us this," I asked. "Who are you buying the cheats from?"

Again he licked his lips. "I dunno. I never got the guy's name."

"How did you contact him?" Chase asked.

"Texts," Chris said. "I asked around, and this senior gave me a phone number. I just texted the guy with what test answers I wanted, and he told me to drop the money here. He said he'd put the answers on a flash drive and swap it for the cash."

In the distance, we could hear the sound of the crowd roaring. From the cheers, it sounded like HHH had made a touchdown. Chris looked from Chase to me.

"You have to believe me. I'm just an innocent consumer in all this."

I shot him a look. *Innocent* was a relative word.

"There's one way to prove that," Chase said. "Empty your pockets."

Chris nodded, then proceeded to turn the pockets of his jeans inside out for inspection. They were empty, as promised. The only things remaining in his sweatshirt pocket were his wallet (containing a student ID, a driver's license, and three dollars in cash) and a set of keys attached to a chain with the eBay logo on it.

"See, I told you. I put the cash under the rock. I'm just the payer, not the payee."

Chase didn't answer. Instead, he kept one hand on Chris's shirt as he led him back to the rock.

Whatever cash Chris had deposited was gone. In its place was a small black flash drive.

"He must have come and gone while we . . ." I looked at Chris.

"While we chased you down," Chase finished, his teeth still gritted together.

"Sorry?" Chris said.

I felt my spirits sink as fast as my muddy heels when I realized I'd squatted in the bushes for nothing.

Chase picked up the drive, turning it over in his hands.

"These must be the test answers," he said.

Chris reached out a hand to take the drive, but Chase quickly slipped it into his pocket.

"Oh, come on!" Chris protested.

But Chase got right up in his face, his voice low and menacing. "If you get caught cheating, not only are you going to be suspended, but I'm losing a staff member from my paper, which I cannot afford to have happen."

Chris gulped, his Adam's apple bobbing up and down as he took a small step backward.

But Chase wasn't done with him. He took another step forward, his eyes narrowing. "So far, your only crime is being stupid enough to give this guy a wad of cash. Which means I have no reason to turn you in to the administration."

Chris's shoulders sagged with relief.

"But," Chase continued, "if I find out that you have actually used stolen answers to cheat on a test? I have no choice but to tell the vice principal. Got it?"

Chris swallowed again. "Yeah," he squeaked out, his voice an octave higher.

"Good." Chase finally backed off. "Now you'd better

get back to the game. Because I expect a finished article on our victory over Saratoga in my in-box first thing Monday morning."

Chris nodded. "Yep. Right. Cool. I'm on it," he said, then scuttled off toward the bright lights of the stadium.

I watched him go, feeling the disappointment of our busted evening.

"Now what do we do?" I asked. "We totally missed the guy selling cheats."

"Now," said Chase, "there's only one thing left to do."

I almost hated to ask. . . .

"What?"

"Set up a sting."

SEVEN

"SO, HOW WAS THE DATE WITH CHASE?" SAM ASKED THE
next afternoon as she pulled her American Government
book from her backpack.

"Stakeout," I corrected, mirroring her actions and
adding a notebook to the pile of studying materials on her
bed.

"Bummer." She paused. "Did Chase even mention your
outfit?"

I fought down heat in my cheeks as I answered. "Yes.
And I am never going out looking like that again."

"Why? You looked hot."

"I looked like a girl who thought she was going out with
a guy and ended up on a stakeout, squatting in the mud in
a pair of heels and smelling like jasmine! I felt ridiculous."

"Oh." Sam bit her lip. "Sorry. I was just kinda hoping

you guys would get together."

"God, why?" I asked, trying to ignore the blast of embarrassment still coursing through me.

Sam shrugged. "I know how uncomfortable you get around Kyle and me."

I bit my lip. Was I that obvious? "You guys aren't that bad."

"I just thought it would be fun to double-date. Then maybe our kissing and stuff wouldn't squick you out so much."

"Thanks." I shot her a smile. "But I'm not squicked. You guys are fine."

"Cool," she said, grinning back at me as she reached into a drawer in her desk and came out with a pencil, pad of paper, and an eraser, all in a matching purple desk set.

My school supplies, on the other hand, consisted of a beat-up spiral-bound notebook and a number two pencil with bite marks on the end.

While Sam is my best friend, her bedroom could not look more different from mine. My walls were a blank eggshell, the same color that had been there when Mom and I had moved in, and were covered in posters and photos ripped from fashion magazines. I had a corkboard tacked to the wall, where pictures of Sam and me were attached with different-colored tacks, and a full-length mirror on the other side of the room. I had a desk, somewhere, but it had been a while since I'd actually used it as a desk—more often it just doubled as a place to put clothes from the overflow of my closet. My bed was rarely made, school papers kind of lived where there was a surface to put them down, and the overall appearance was lived-in.

Sam's room, in contrast, looked like an ad from Pottery Barn. The walls were pale violet, to go with the bedspread on her perfectly made bed, and all her furniture matched: a white clapboard look dominating the headboard, dresser, and desk. Above the desk in the corner was a board covered in quilted fabric with ribbons running diagonally across it to keep photos in place (a couple of them copies of the ones on my board at home), and every drawer, cubbyhole, and cupboard was perfectly ordered inside and out with organizers of every size.

And, for as much as Sam was into fashion, I didn't see a stray piece of clothing anywhere.

Sam was like my tidy evil twin.

I shifted on her bed, almost afraid to make a wrinkle as I flipped my binder open to my American Government notes.

"So how did the stakeout go?" Sam asked.

"Terrible." I shoved my book bag onto the floor then filled Sam in on the Chris fiasco.

"And by the time we got back to the rock," I finished, "the cash was gone. We'd totally missed him."

"Wow," Sam said, shaking her head. "Chris Fret. I never would have figured him for a cheater. He always seemed so . . . normal."

"Yeah, well, apparently 'normal' also means too busy to study for a quiz."

"You know," Sam said, scrunching up her face, "it's totally unfair to those of us who are struggling to get those good grades. I mean, take this American Government midterm we have coming up. How many people do you think already have the answers to that? Mr. Bleaker grades on a curve, you know. Those cheaters are ruining the curve for the rest of us."

I had to agree—it sucked big elephant balls.

"Not only that," Sam went on, "but we have to compete against these cheaters to get into good colleges. Chris is my Stanford competition. How can I compete with someone who's buying all the fudging answers?"

I raised an eyebrow at her. "'Fudging'?"

"What? You liked 'fluffin'' better?"

I shrugged. "Either way, I don't think Chris is much competition for you, stolen answers or no," I said, recalling our encounter.

"So, what do we do now?" Sam asked.

"Well . . ." I hedged. "Chase had an idea last night."

"What?" Sam asked.

"He thought we should set up a sting. Try to catch

the guy in action again."

Sam nodded. "Sounds like a reasonable plan."

"Only, we're going to need someone to contact him about getting test answers."

"Right."

"And it can't be me or Chase because everyone already knows we're working on the story for the paper."

"True."

"So we're going to need a third person to make the contact with the guy selling cheats."

"Good point. But it could be hard to find someone willing to do that."

I stared pointedly at Sam.

She blinked back at me. "What?"

I bit my lip and stared some more.

Realization slowly dawned behind her brown eyes. "Oh no. Oh, no way, Hartley. I am not going to be your bait!"

"Please, Sam," I pleaded. "You're perfect. Everyone knows how grade-driven you are, and you said yourself that we're in trouble with the midterm coming up in American Government."

Sam shook her head so violently that her blond hair whipped at her cheeks. "No way. Big capital N-O. What if I get caught? Teachers are totally looking for cheaters now with the whole Sydney thing. I cannot get caught cheating!"

"You won't get caught," I assured her. "You're not actually going to cheat. We're just buying the answers. Heck, you won't even see the answers. If all goes well, we'll catch this guy in the act of grabbing the money before he even has a chance to drop the flash drive."

Sam bit her lip. "This feels like a really bad idea, Hartley."

My turn to shake my head. "No. It feels like a really good story. A good story that I need to jump on now before someone else does," I said, remembering Ashley's total ton of hits. "And one that no one else is pursuing because everyone thinks Sydney killed herself. Her killer's going to go free to commit Twittercide again unless we figure out who he is," I pointed out, trying to butter her up with her own phrase. "Please, Sam. For Sydney?"

Sam clenched her jaw. Then she finally threw her hands up. "Okay, fine. I'll be your bait."

"Thank you!" I squealed, coming in for a hug.

"But," she said quickly, "if I get caught, I'm so pulling a Sydney and ratting you out to save my own GPA."

I nodded. "Deal. Fine. You rock, Sam."

"Yeah," she said, grabbing her cell phone. "Let's just hope I don't rock it all the way to fudging suspension. What's the guy's number?"

I rattled off the digits that I'd extracted from Chris last night and watched as Sam punched them into her phone.

"What should I say?" Sam asked, turning to me.

"Hmm." I thought a second. "Say that you got his number from a friend."

Sam nodded, texting as I dictated.

"And that you have too many honors classes to keep up right now. You need the answers to Bleaker's American Government midterm."

I watched Sam's thumbs fly across the mini keyboard as the words appeared on the small screen. I reread it over her shoulder, then we hit Send.

"How long do you think it will take to hear back?" Sam asked.

I shrugged. "Let's hope not long."

We settled in to do our American Government homework together (if we weren't really going to cheat, we did really need to study) and waited, Sam checking her phone every couple of minutes to make sure we hadn't missed him.

About twenty minutes later, just as we were going over the checks and balances system, Sam's cell buzzed. We both jumped off the bed and dove for it. The text was from our mystery cheat seller, and Sam quickly opened it, both of us reading off the screen.

$50. drop under rock by mascot room friday b4 game. answers will b there @ 1/2time.

I shook my head. "We can't wait that long. The

midterm's Friday. Tell him you need the answers today in order to have time to memorize them for the test."

Sam complied, texting back. She hit Send and we both waited, staring at the blank screen. Three minutes later, a response buzzed in. Sam punched it open and we leaned forward to read the message.

2 soon. need more time

I pursed my lips together. "Tell him you'll pay double for a rush job."

Sam raised her eyebrows at me. "And where are we going to get a hundred bucks?"

"Don't worry about that. Just type it."

She shrugged, then did.

will pay $100 for answers 2day

A minute later, our response came in:

2morrow. oakridge mall. 1pm. $100 under the kangaroo's paw at the kids playland.

Yes!

Commence Operation Stakeout: the Sequel.

By the time Sam and I finished studying and I walked the mile and a half from her place to my house, it was starting to get dark. I found Mom at the kitchen table once again, laptop open, eyes glued to the screen.

"Hey, Hartley," she said, still not looking up. "That you?"

"Yeah." I dropped my book bag on the floor and followed the scents of dinner into the kitchen. "What's cooking?" I pulled the top off a pot on the back stove burner, leaning in to smell.

"Lentil and quinoa stew," Mom answered.

I wrinkled my nose, wondering what the chances were I could sneak a pizza upstairs instead.

"Hey, come look at this guy on Match and tell me what you think."

Oh boy. I could tell her what I thought without looking—nothing good could come of Mom internet dating.

"Uh, wow. You know I have a lot of studying to do. . . ."

"I thought you were studying at Sam's."

"I have a lot more studying to do."

"This will only take a sec," Mom said, hailing me over. "Come look at this guy's profile."

Clearly I was not getting out of this, so I did glance at the screen. In the upper left-hand corner was a picture of a guy with graying hair and kind of a crooked smile. He was standing on the beach with a yellow dog next to him.

"What do you think?" Mom asked.

I shrugged. "He seems kinda old, doesn't he? I mean, gray hair?"

"He's not that old," Mom said, cocking her head to the side. "He's just a little salt and pepper. And his profile sounds very nice," she said, indicating the paragraph of description under the "about me" section.

I scrolled down. "He says he likes long walks on the beach," I read, rolling my eyes. "Cheesy."

"What's wrong with the beach? I like the beach," Mom said.

I frowned at her. "And 'holding hands at sunset' and 'candlelit dinners.'"

"So?"

"Mom! How cliché is that?"

"It's not cliché," she argued. "It's romantic."

I made a fake gagging motion.

"All right, enough. Don't you have studying to do?" Mom said, making a shooing motion at me.

Thank God for midterms.

EIGHT

THE NEXT MORNING, I WOKE UP WITH ONE THING ON MY mind: how to get one hundred dollars and fast.

Unfortunately, the only job I'd ever had was babysitting neighborhood kids, and even if I scared up a couple little guys to watch on short notice, no way could I make one hundred dollars in one sitting. Ditto Sam. Her parents didn't allow her to have an after-school job, thinking it would interfere too much with her studies.

That left us with precious few options to earn money in time for the drop. We would either have to (A) steal it or (B) borrow it. Since neither of us were the larceny type, Sunday morning found us standing in front of Sam's brother, Kevin, pleading our case for a short-term loan.

"I promise we won't even spend it. We just need to use it as bait for a couple hours, then we'll bring it right back," Sam told him.

Kevin blinked, giving her a blank stare. Though come to think of it, Kevin always had kind of a blank stare on his face. He was dressed in jeans and a faded Green Day T-shirt, laid out on the sofa with one foot hooked over the end in a sprawling pose. The TV was showing some nature channel with a bunch of ocean scenes, and the coffee table in front of him was littered with an empty Cap'n Crunch box and half a pepperoni pizza.

"Dude, a hundred bucks is a lot of money," Kevin said. "You know how many boobies I could save with a hundred bucks?"

I almost hated to ask. . . . "Boobies?"

Kevin nodded. "There are only like a dozen Abbott's Boobies left in the world. The whole world, dude! That's, like, really not a lot."

"Birds?"

Kevin nodded solemnly. "Endangered birds, dude. They're being killed off by Yellow Crazy Ants."

Clearly someone had been watching way too much Nature Channel.

"Look, we'll do anything, Kev. Please? We really need the money," Sam pleaded.

Kevin raised one eyebrow. "Anything?"

Uh-oh. "Um, well, maybe not anything—" I broke in.

"Okay, how about this?" Kevin proposed. "There's this job I'm supposed to do this afternoon. It pays a hundred and fifty dollars, and if you two wanna do it for me, you can keep the cash."

"What kind of job?" I asked. As far as I knew, Kevin's only real job since graduating from high school two years ago had been keeping the Kramers' sofa from floating away.

"Just a quick one."

I narrowed my eyes. "This job is legal, right?"

Kevin did a short laugh-slash-cough thing. "Totally, dude. Look, all you have to do is stand in front of Chuck's Chicken on Main Street and hand out chicken bucket coupons for a couple hours. Easy, right?"

I had to admit, it did sound easy.

"I don't know," Sam hedged. "Main Street is like three miles away."

"You can take the Green Machine," he offered, sweetening the deal.

I bit my lip. The Green Machine was Kevin's puke-green-colored Volvo sedan that was, in fact, an environmentally friendly "green" machine by virtue of the fact that it ran purely on clean-burning vegetable oil instead of fossil fuels. Though the term *clean* was relative. The only places that had the volume of veggie oil needed to run a car were fast-food joints that threw out drums of used cooking oil. Which meant the Green Machine perpetually smelled like French fries and fish sticks.

But, while I had a moment of pause over being seen driving around town in Kevin's car, the truth was if we wanted to catch our cheat seller and figure out who killed Sydney, we had little choice.

"Okay," I finally said. "We'll do it."

Kevin grinned, showing off a piece of pepperoni stuck in his back teeth. "Sweet, dude. The gig starts in an hour, and the suit's in the Green Machine's backseat."

I paused. "Wait—suit? What suit?"

Kevin blinked at me. "The chicken suit, dude. You didn't think you could hand out coupons looking like that, did you?"

I closed my eyes and did a mental two count while I yoga-breathed, telling myself that this was all for a good cause.

Forty minutes later, Sam and I were parking the Green Machine at Chuck's Chicken in a haze of fried food–flavored smoke. Sam cut the engine, and we got out and stared into the backseat. Laid out across the cracked vinyl bench was a huge mass of yellow feathers.

I bit my lip. "So . . ."

"Yeah, no way," Sam said, reading my mind. "I'm so not being a giant chicken, Hartley."

"It's just for a couple hours."

"N. O."

"I think the feathers match your hair color better than mine."

"Nice try. We have the same color hair, Hartley."

"I'm allergic to feathers?"

"Liar."

"I'm allergic to looking like a dork?"

Sam grinned. "Ditto. Besides, I'm already putting my academic reputation on the line to buy these cheats."

She had a point. "Fine." I sighed. "I'll be the chicken." So not words I'd ever wanted to say in my life.

Reluctantly, I picked up the suit and held it up. Yellow feathers covered the torso, wings sticking out the sides with little arm holes for my hands. A pair of orange stockings attached to huge webbed feet covered the bottom half, and a hat with a mass of yellow fuzz sticking into the air capped off the outfit.

I gave Sam one last pleading look.

"You sure you don't want to wear the suit?"

"I've never been so sure of anything in my life."

"Sigh," I said out loud.

"Tell you what," she offered, taking pity on me, "you can keep the extra fifty bucks."

"Swell."

I took the suit into the bathroom of Chuck's Chicken, and after maneuvering uncomfortably in the tiny metal stall (and almost dunking my tail feathers into the toilet), I finally had the thing on. I purposely did not look in the mirror on my way out, sucking up the odd looks and snickers from the patrons enjoying their fried poultry and biscuits as I walked back out through the restaurant to find the manager.

He turned out to be a short Indian guy with a pinched nose and a unibrow hunkering down over his eyes in a frown.

"You're not Kevin," he observed, squinting past the costume to look at my face.

I shook my head, molting a few yellow feathers onto the floor in the process. "He couldn't make it. He sent me instead."

The manager paused, gave my suit a scrutinizing stare, then shrugged. "Whatever. Here, just hand these out to people on the street."

He handed me a stack of coupons.

"And try to dance around a little," he added. "You know, attract attention."

Trust me, there was no way I wouldn't attract attention. An older couple in the corner was laughing behind their palms, two junior high kids were openly staring, and one toddler was asking Mom if she could go hug Big Bird.

I grabbed the coupons and trudged outside to find Sam already sitting on the curb outside the restaurant. She took one look at me and grinned. Then pulled out her phone.

"You wouldn't."

"Just one little picture. Just to send to Kyle."

I rolled my eyes. Sending "one little picture" to Kyle was

like cc'ing the entire world. If you Wikipedia-ed *gossip*, I'm pretty sure Kyle's face popped up. "If this ends up on YouTube, I'm totally disowning you as my best friend," I warned.

Sam just grinned wider. "Say 'feathers,'" she said, snapping a photo.

An hour later, my stack of coupons was gone, taking my dignity with it. I stripped off the molting suit and put my street clothes back on before collecting our payment from the manager. Then we jumped back into the Green Machine and headed for the mall, where we were supposed to drop the money in half an hour.

After circling only ten minutes for a parking spot (and stalking a woman with a Macy's shopping bag all the way from the door to her red sedan), we made our way inside and toward the back corner of the mall.

The kid's playland was an enclosed area full of slides, climbing equipment, toy cars, and little puzzles all made out of foam where the under-four-foot set could run wild between Mom's shopping sprees. Everything was rounded and owie-free, including the giant six-foot-tall foam kangaroo guarding the entrance.

Sam acted as lookout as I slipped the hundred bucks I'd made playing chicken under the back left paw of the kangaroo, then we both took a seat on a bench across the walkway to wait.

And wait.

And wait.

Fifteen minutes later, no one had touched the paw.

Sam squirmed in the seat beside me.

"Hey, how long do you think this is gonna take?" she asked.

I shook my head. "I don't know." Honestly, I'd hoped the guy would have been there by then. "Why?" I asked.

Sam pulled her cell from her pocket, checking the time. "I have a tutoring appointment in an hour and a half."

"I didn't know you had a tutor."

She nodded. "She's helping me study for the SATs."

I turned to her. "Sam, SATs aren't until May."

"My dad believes in being prepared."

Clearly.

I glanced at the kangaroo, still standing by his lonely self. "Go," I said.

She raised an eyebrow at me.

"Just go. I'll wait and watch for our cheat seller. I don't want you to miss tutoring," I said, even though the fact that our cheat seller was also likely a killer made me kinda shudder at the idea of facing him alone.

Sam looked at her cell readout again. She pursed her lips. I could see a serious mental debate waging in the crease between her eyebrows. But finally, she put her phone away and shook her head.

"No. I'm not leaving you alone. What if he tries to run,

like Chris? You're gonna need backup."

I gave her a quick hug. "Thanks." As much as I didn't want her to get in trouble for missing tutoring, I was definitely glad she was staying. Truth? I had no idea what I was doing. I totally needed backup.

We settled in to silence again as we watched kids filter in and out of the playland, tired parents in tow. No one stopped at the kangaroo. Well, once a curly-haired little blond boy shouted at it and tried to bite its tail, but that was about it.

I was just about to give up and concede that he wasn't coming when a girl in a hot pink tank made her way to the entrance to playland.

Without a kid.

She had her back to us, so I couldn't see her face, but from where we sat, I could tell she was about our age. Her hair was stick straight blond shot through with pale pink highlights, and she had on black skinny jeans, black slouching boots, and about a dozen silver bracelets on each wrist.

She walked into the playland, then did a quick look over both shoulders before crouching down (with difficulty, due to the tight jeans), next to Mr. Kangaroo's back left paw.

Bingo.

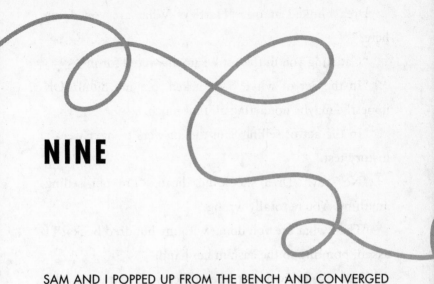

NINE

SAM AND I POPPED UP FROM THE BENCH AND CONVERGED on the girl. She stood and turned to go, and I recognized her face immediately. Drea Barlow.

Drea was a cheerleader at our school, which meant she was constantly walking that fine line between sophisticated and slutty. Tight clothes, thick eyeliner, and padded bras were the uniform of all cheerleaders at our school, both on and off the field. Half the squad had tattoos, 90 percent had eating disorders, and every year they lost at least two of their ranks to unplanned pregnancies where serious calculations were needed just to figure paternity.

While Drea was the last person I expected to be clever enough to be selling the cheats, her moral standards were just about right.

"Busted," I said as Sam and I approached her.

Drea blinked at me. "Hartley? What are you doing here?"

"Catching you in the act," Sam answered for me.

"In the act of what?" she asked, playing dumb. Or, honestly, maybe not acting all that much.

"In the act of selling Sam the answers to next week's history test."

"No way." Drea shook her head. "I'm not selling anything. You're totally wrong."

"Then what are you doing with my hundred bucks?" I asked, pointing to the cash in her hand.

She looked down at it, then quickly shoved it into the back pocket of her jeans. Or it would have been quickly if they hadn't been painted on. These were beyond skinny jeans. They were like a denim wet suit. She wiggled a little, struggling to hide the evidence as she continued shaking her head. "I found that money."

"We watched you walk right to it," Sam pointed out.

Drea bit her lip. "So? I can walk wherever I want. It's a free country."

I gave her a "get real" look.

"Get real," Sam said, not content to stick with just a look. "Drea, you knew the money would be there because you're the one who told us to put it there."

She shrugged. "Prove it."

Sam narrowed her eyes at her. "Fine." Then she pulled

her cell from her pocket and dialed the number we'd texted our request to yesterday. I heard it ring three times on Sam's end, but the phone I could clearly see outlined in Drea's right front pocket remained conspicuously silent.

"See?" Drea said with a smirk. "I'm innocent. Now, if you don't mind, I have things to do." Then she brushed past us, making a beeline down the mall.

Sam moved to stop her, but I put a hand on her arm.

"Wait," I whispered as we watched Drea's boots clomp away. "Let's follow her."

Sam raised an eyebrow. "Why?"

"Clearly Drea is not the sharpest crayon in the box."

"Clearly."

"Which means she's probably picking up the cash for whoever is really behind selling the cheats."

"Like a mastermind?"

I shot her a look. "Are we in an Austin Powers movie?"

Sam shrugged. "What? It's a very accurate description."

I had to admit, it kinda was.

I nodded as Drea turned the corner at the Orange Julius. "Fine. A mastermind. Now come on. Let's see where she goes."

Sam and I jogged past the Orange Julius, then peeked around a potted palm tree. Drea was paused in front of the Forever 21, three stores down. We watched as she checked out the window display, then walked inside.

Sam and I quickly ran to the front of the store, then slipped inside and ducked behind a rack of "flirty cap-sleeve" Ts.

"What's she doing?" I asked as Sam peeked around the side shelf.

"She's looking at the earrings," Sam whispered back. "Now she's checking out a belt . . . and a matching cuff bracelet."

Fabulous. Drea was on a shopping detour.

"Is she meeting anyone? Talking to anyone?"

Sam craned her neck around a pile of clothes. "She just said something to the salesperson, but I think it was about the bracelet's price tag." She paused. "I think it might be on sale."

I rolled my eyes. "What's she doing now?"

"Checking out a sweater. . . . Oh, it's really cute. I wonder if that's on sale."

"Focus, Sam," I said, but I couldn't help peeking around the display. She was right. It was a cute sweater. I made a mental note to come back later.

Unfortunately, I watched as Drea took the sweater and headed back toward the dressing rooms.

"This is pointless," I decided. "Let's go." I nodded toward the door, and we slunk out of the store.

"Now what?" Sam asked.

I shrugged. "I guess we wait for her to finish shopping."

Sam nodded, her gaze slowly surveying the mall. "I'm gonna get a Julius. Want one?"

I shook my head. "I'll keep watch," I offered, gesturing to Forever 21.

Five minutes later, Sam came back with a smoothie, a pretzel, and a carton of chili cheese fries.

"Dude."

Sam blinked at me. "What? I haven't had lunch."

"Didn't I see you down a chicken platter at Chuck's?"

She shrugged. "That was a mid-morning snack. Besides," she said, shoving a fry in her mouth. "I have a lacrosse game later. I need my strength."

I would have argued that chili cheese fries were hardly the lunch of champions, but out of the corner of my eye I saw Drea leaving Forever 21 with a plastic shopping bag in hand.

I elbowed Sam in the ribs. "Let's go."

We did, following her at a pace of three stores back as she walked toward the center of the mall. She paused again outside Hot Topic, slipping inside. I followed (leaving Sam outside the store to down her feast), ducking around displays as I watched Drea grab a micromini and head for a dressing room.

Four outfits later, she finally made a purchase and headed back out again.

I let her get ahead, lingering near the wall of T-shirts

with cartoon characters spouting inappropriate slogans (at least that's how my mom would characterize them—I actually thought a couple were kinda funny), then slipped back outside to find Sam hot on Drea's tail four stores down.

Unfortunately, we only got a few feet before Drea ducked into Pacific Sun and started eyeing bikinis.

Half an hour later, Sam's meal was a thing of the past, she'd sucked the last of her smoothie, and Drea had taken us on a tour of pretty much the entire mall.

"Maybe she's not meeting the seller today," Sam suggested.

"Maybe he's just late."

"Maybe she really did just find the cash. Or maybe she saw us put it there and decided to take it."

I pursed my lips together, really not liking that theory. "Five more minutes. If she doesn't lead us anywhere by then, we'll call it a bust."

Sam nodded, eyeing the Cold Stone Creamery to our right as we followed Drea toward the food court. "Maybe I should get some dessert. . . ." She trailed off.

"There!" I said, pointing to Drea and grabbing Sam by the arm.

I felt my heart leap into my throat as I watched Drea sit down at a table near the Panda Express, where a guy in a black wool beanie cap was eating chow mein. She leaned in and gave him a quick kiss on the lips before pulling something from her back pocket and sliding it across the table.

I sucked in a breath. Our cash.

"Holy fudge, that's the guy!" Sam whispered in my ear. "Let's go get him."

We quickly converged on the table, and as we approached, I saw Drea look up, first shock, then anger registering on her face.

"What are you two doing here?" she asked, narrowing heavily lined eyes until there was nothing but mascara showing.

"Catching you red-handed," Sam said, pointing at the guy with her.

He looked up, and I recognized him from school. I didn't know his name, but I'd seen him in the halls. He had dark eyes, dark longish hair, and a perpetual summer tan. He was wearing a green T-shirt and jeans, his long legs stretched out in front of him under the table to end in a pair of black skate shoes that looked well worn in. He looked from me to Sam.

"Caught who doing what?" he asked, blinking innocently.

"Caught Drea bringing you the cash for the cheats we purchased. From you," Sam said, still pointing a finger at the guy.

He looked from Sam to me. "I'm not sure I know what you're talking about."

"Oh, come off it, Nicky," Sam said, plopping herself into an empty seat across from the guy. Apparently she did recognize him.

"Nicky?" I asked, sitting down, too.

Sam turned to me. "This is Nicky Williams. He's in my AP English class. And," she said, giving him a pointed look, "he was in Mr. Tipkins's precalculus class last year, too."

Nicky shrugged. "A lot of people have had Tipkins."

"A lot of people didn't just send their flunkey to pick up cash from the kids' playland."

"Hey!" Drea protested. "I'll have you know I'm not flunking any subjects this semester."

I rolled my eyes.

Nicky, on the other hand, ignored his girlfriend's lack of IQ. His eyes went from Sam to me again. "You're the girl who found Sydney, right?"

"Yes. I'm doing a story for the school paper on her death."

He nodded slowly. "Yeah. That really sucked."

"Sucks losing *customers*, huh?" Sam said.

Nicky grinned and crossed his arms over his chest. "Customers? Gosh, I'm sorry. I really don't know what you're talking about."

The mock innocence thing was getting old. I grabbed Sam's phone from her pocket and dialed the number of our seller.

Immediately, the Black Eyed Peas starting singing from Nicky's pocket.

Nicky bit the inside of his cheek, not bothering to pull his phone out as I shot him a pointed look.

"Okay, fine," he conceded. "Look, you wanna know about Sydney? I'll talk. Off the record," he added.

As much as I didn't like the sound of that, I nodded. Better than no talk at all.

"Fine. Off the record."

"What do you want to know?"

"You are the guy we texted last night?" Sam asked.

He nodded. "Yeah."

"And you're selling cheats to people at school?"

Again with the nod.

"Did you sell the cheats to Sydney Sanders?"

He paused this time before answering. "She was in a jam. I helped her out."

"For a fee."

"A guy's gotta eat, ya know?" he said, gesturing to the pile of chow mein in front of him.

"Where did you get the answers?"

"I have a source."

"What kind of source?" Sam asked.

"The kind I'm not gonna talk about. Next question," he said, nodding my way.

"Fine," I said, switching gears. "How many people at Herbert Hoover High are involved in this?" I asked.

"How many have I sold to?" he asked. "Maybe a dozen this semester."

Sam whistled low. "That's it. I'm never getting into Stanford now."

"And none of those people know who you are? It's all been anonymous?" I asked, ignoring her.

"Yep."

"Did Sydney know who you were?"

Nicky shook his head. "No. No one did."

"Is it possible she found out about your 'source'?" I asked.

Nicky narrowed his eyes at me. "Why do you ask?"

Unlike Drea, I could tell he was no dummy. So, with little left to lose, I leveled with him.

"Sydney was going to tell me something important the day she died."

"Like what?"

"I don't know. She died before she could tell me. But I assume it had something to do with where she got the cheats."

Nicky shook his head. "Look, if it did, it had nothing to do with me. Sydney dropped the cash. I dropped the drive with the answers. That's it. She was clueless. Trust me."

Despite his suggestion, that wasn't something I was totally prepared to do yet.

"Where were you the afternoon that Sydney died?" I asked instead.

"What do you mean?"

"I mean, do you have an alibi?"

"Whoa!" Nicky put both hands out in a defensive gesture. "Sydney committed suicide, right? What do I need an alibi for?"

"We don't think it was suicide. We think it was homicide."

Sam nodded in agreement beside me. "Twittercide, to be exact."

"Well, it wasn't me," Nicky said defiantly.

"Then where were you?"

"Home."

"On a school day?" I asked, raising an eyebrow at him.

"I was sick. I had a cold."

"Can anyone vouch for that?" I asked.

"Drea can," Nicky said, nodding across the table at the girl who'd been conspicuously silent during our exchange. "She stopped by before school to check on me."

"Before school," I said, honing in on the word. "So, when Sydney died after school you were alone."

Nicky bit his lip. "I guess. So what?"

"So maybe you thought Sydney knew too much and needed to be shut up before she blew the whistle on your whole operation," Sam offered.

He shook his head. "No way. Like I said, Sydney didn't know who she was buying the cheats from."

"Are you sure about that?" I asked, narrowing my eyes at him. "Because it wasn't all that hard for us to find out."

He paused, looking from me to Sam, letting the truth of that sink in. "Anyway, even if she did know, she wouldn't tell."

"She ratted out her best friend," Sam pointed out.

"Look, I told you I was sick. I had a fever. I couldn't have killed Sydney that day even if I wanted to."

"Then where was Drea at three thirty?" I asked, turning on the cheerleader.

"Me?" she squeaked out. "Why would I want to hurt Sydney?"

"Why did you pick up the cash for Nicky today?" I countered. "Maybe he told you to do another little favor for him and silence Sydney."

Drea paled beneath her layers of makeup. "Nicky would never ask me to do that. He's a sweetheart."

"A sweetheart who sells illegal cheats."

"But he doesn't hurt anyone!" Drea protested.

"Ha!" Sam countered. "You think messing with a

grading curve is a victimless crime? I'm pulling an A-minus average this semester. A-minus!"

"Dude," Nicky said, putting his hands out in front of him again. "Enough. I didn't kill Sydney and neither did Drea, okay? Period. End of story."

Only it did not feel like end of story to me. "Look, you can either tell us where you were," I warned, "or we can turn you in to the police and you can talk to them."

Nicky put his hands palms up. "Turn me in for what? I haven't done anything."

"Seriously?" Sam asked, putting her hands on her hips.

Nicky grinned. "Well, anything that you can prove. I'll deny everything I just told you."

"What about the cash?" I asked.

"Drea found it. Plain and simple."

"Quite a coincidence."

"What were you doing buying cheats anyway?" Nicky said, giving Sam a pointed look.

"It was for a story!"

"Says you."

"Wait—what do you mean 'says you'?" Sam asked nervously.

"Anything you say is your word against mine. You turn me in, I turn Sam in to the vice principal for trying to cheat. Dig?"

Sam narrowed her eyes at Nicky, thinking all sorts

of dirty words if I could read them correctly. "You fluff-eating son of a monkey with a rash up his—"

"Fine," I said, breaking in before Sam could get any more creative. "I guess we'll just have to find your 'source' another way."

Nicky shrugged, then leaned back in his seat and dropped a chow mien noodle into his smug mouth. "Good luck with that, girls."

I hated to admit that he was right. We were in serious need of some luck.

TEN

"I GUESS NICKY'S A DEAD END," SAM OBSERVED AS WE walked back through the mall.

"Agreed." Unfortunately. "But maybe we need to look at this a different way."

"Such as?"

"Well, what if Nicky's right and Sydney didn't know who was giving Nicky the test answers?"

She frowned. "Okay. But then who killed her?"

"Sydney being caught cheating affected other people. What if her murder—"

"Twittercide," Sam supplied.

"Right. What if her Twittercide wasn't because of the cheating itself but fallout from getting caught?"

"Like a pissed-off former BFF?," Sam asked.

I nodded. "Quinn had good reason to be mad at

Sydney, true, but she also had a pretty good alibi. On the other hand, I can think of at least one other person who might not have been happy about Sydney being kicked off the homecoming court. Her boyfriend."

Sam's eyes lit up. "Totally! Connor and Sydney were shoo-ins for king and queen."

"But with Sydney out of the running, Connor was pretty much out of it, too," I said. "Which he might not have been too happy about."

"Unhappy enough to kill?" Sam asked.

I nodded. "Let's go find out."

Connor Crane was captain of the soccer team and starting quarterback for the football team. Luckily he was also on the water polo team with Kyle, who texted Connor's number to Sam, who then texted Connor, who said he was at work but would meet us at Nickel City in two hours.

Which was just enough time for Sam to get to her tutoring appointment. Sam and I coughed the Green Machine up to Do the Math! Tutoring only forty minutes behind schedule. Sam rushed in to conquer calculus while I waited in the car. I wished I'd taken the time to grab something to eat at the food court before we left, as the scent of fried smoke was making me hungry. Instead, I pulled out my phone and texted Chase, updating him on our interview with Nicky.

where did he get the cheats? he asked once I'd
finished.

he wont say.

guesses?

I leaned back in the vinyl seat, feeling my forehead
crease in thought as I looked out the window and watched
a squirrel scuttle across the tutor's parking lot.

he had drea pick up cash 4 him. mayB he had
someone else stealing the cheats 4 him.

There was a pause, then Chase texted back.

doesn't like 2 do dirty work himself?

doesn't like 2 get caught. he's crooked but smart.

next step? Chase asked.

going 2 see BF connor @ Nckle CiT. mayB syd's
death unrel8d to cheats.

I could feel Chase contemplating this angle in the
silence on the other end. Finally he sent back,

i'll meet u there. time?

I texted back and agreed to meet up in an hour. I could
only hope that Connor was a little more forthcoming than
Nicky had been.

Nickel City was an arcade where for five cents you could
play any video game in the place. The catch? They were all
vintage oldies. As was the building. The floors were slightly
sticky from countless spilled sodas, the walls smelled

like stale pizza, and the arcade consoles themselves were chipped, faded, and slick where sweaty palms had clutched joysticks in hundreds of death grips.

As soon as we walked in the door, I spied Chase waiting for us next to an ancient Ms. Pac-Man machine.

"Hey," he said. "Connor's over there playing Gran Turismo." He gestured to a machine along the back wall.

"You talk to him yet?" I asked.

He shook his head. "Waiting for you two."

"Let's do it," Sam said, striding toward him. Chase and I followed a step behind.

"Hey," he said, leaning in. "No jasmine today, huh?"

I ducked my head as I walked. "I told you it was the bushes."

"Bummer. They were nice-smelling bushes."

I ignored the comment (and the blush it created in my cheeks), instead focusing on Connor.

With blond hair, blue eyes, and zero acne, Connor Crane was currently the secret crush of half the female HHH population. And a couple of the males, too.

Personally, I'd always thought there was something just a little too perfect about him. His look was as carefully planned as the dressed mannequins in the Abercrombie windows—each hair of his casual messy-do gelled into place with precision to look carelessly cool, his outfits meticulously chosen to look like he'd just pulled something random from his closet. It was the kind of effortless look that everyone knew required a lot of effort.

"Connor," I called as we approached his game console.

"Hey," he replied, though he didn't look up from his screen, furiously pressing buttons and twisting the plastic steering wheel.

"Can we talk to you for a sec?"

"Sure." But he still didn't look up.

"Uh . . . maybe face to face?"

"Hang on a sec," he said, punctuating his words with a slam to the B button. I watched as his car careened over an oil slick on the road, skidding sideways, then slamming into an invisible wall. Finally his vehicle raced over the finish line and the words *Game Over* appeared.

Connor scowled at the screen.

"Um, got a minute now?" I asked.

Connor looked up for the first time, seeming a little surprised to find us there.

"Oh. Right. Sure." He crossed his arms over his chest and leaned against the arcade game. "What did you want to talk about?"

"Sydney."

A frown creased between his brows. "What about her?"

"You two were going out, right?" Sam asked.

He looked down at his feet and nodded, kicking at the sticky carpet with one toe. "Were. Past tense. We broke up."

"When?" I asked.

He shrugged again. "Right before she died."

"You mean right after she got caught cheating?" Sam jumped in.

Connor shrugged. "Yeah. So?"

"Why?"

Connor bit his lip and did some more carpet kicking. "You know. Stuff."

Bull-fluff. You didn't break up with a girlfriend of a whole year because of "stuff."

"Did she dump you?" Sam asked, the queen of blunt.

Connor's head snapped up. "No! Dude, girls do not dump me."

I did a mental eye roll but stopped myself just short of actually snorting out loud. Apparently, in addition to being the number one secret crush at our school, Connor *knew* he was the number one secret crush at our school.

"So, you dumped Sydney?" Chase prompted.

Connor looked from Chase to me, then nodded slowly. "Yeah."

"Did it have anything to do with her getting caught cheating?" I asked.

"Kinda," he hedged.

"Or," Sam added, "did it have more to do with her being kicked off the homecoming nomination list, taking you with her?"

The frown between his eyebrows deepened. I'd never noticed until now how thick those eyebrows were. The only not so perfect thing about him.

Well, that and the fact that he may have killed his girlfriend.

"Fine. I dumped her because she got us kicked off. So what?"

"So you must have been pretty pissed off at Sydney about losing homecoming king."

"I wasn't happy about it."

"Unhappy enough to do something about it?" I asked.

Connor narrowed his eyes. "What exactly are you getting at?"

"We don't think Sydney killed herself," Sam said. "We think someone Twittercided her."

Connor cocked his head.

"Killed her," I supplied.

"And you think it was me?" Connor's voice went up an octave.

Sam and I both gave him hard stares.

"Dude!" Connor took another step back. "No way. I did not hurt Sydney. You guys have got this all wrong," he said, turning to Chase.

"So straighten us out," he challenged.

"Look, yes, I was upset at first. Homecoming is a big deal, you know? But just because she was out of the running didn't mean I was."

"People vote on couples," I reminded him.

He grinned. "I am in a couple. I got another girl already."

"That was fast," Sam observed.

"Hey, voting ends Thursday. I didn't have any time to waste. Look, Sydney knew how important homecoming was. So she was cool with me breaking up with her just for the voting and coronation. I promised her that I'd take her back after I was crowned king."

"Wait—so the new girlfriend is just for show?" Sam asked.

Connor nodded. "Right."

"Gee, who's the lucky lady?" I asked, though I was pretty sure my sarcasm was lost on him from the way he puffed his chest out with pride as he answered.

"Jenni Pritchard."

I felt my face do an involuntary scrunch.

Jenni Pritchard was our school's answer to Snooki. Big hair, big boobs, big mouth. She was pulling a solid D average this semester and had failed our last lit assignment when she'd included a description of Keira Knightley's dress in her *Pride and Prejudice* oral book report. The only reason she was even in the running for homecoming queen was that by virtue of her big mouth (and big boobs) everyone in the school knew who Jenni was.

"Wait a minute," Chase said. "Isn't Jenni dating Ben Fisher? I thought I saw their names on the ballot together."

"Was dating Ben Fisher. She broke up with that guy when I asked her out."

"So, let me get this straight," I said, holding up a hand. "You dumped Sydney to steal Jenni away from Ben to win homecoming. Then you were gonna dump Jenni and get back together with Sydney?" I said.

He grinned. "Totally clever, right?"

I rolled my eyes.

But the gesture was lost on Connor, who continued to outline his plan. "No one ever uses the write in option to vote, so when Sydney got kicked off the court, I knew my chances of still winning were better if I was dating someone already on the ballot."

"So, you were planning on getting back together with Sydney, but now that she's dead . . ." Sam trailed off.

Connor shrugged. "I guess I'll stay with Jenni. I mean, at least until winter formal. We have a good chance of king and queen there, too, with Sydney gone."

He was a true romantic.

"Did Jenni know you were planning to dump her for Sydney again after homecoming?"

"No way!" Connor shook his head. "She totally wouldn't have gone for it if she did." He paused. "Wait— you guys aren't, like, friends with her, are you?"

I shook my head and could see him sag with relief.

"Anyway, as you can see, I had no reason to want Sydney dead. I mean, she actually did me a favor by getting kicked off the ballot. My chances of winning are way better with Jenni anyway."

His compassion for the dead girl was overwhelming.

"So, just for the record . . . where were you the afternoon that she died?" Chase asked.

"School," he said. "Then football practice. I didn't even hear she was dead until that night."

I nodded. Dozens of people must have seen him at practice. Still, it would have been pretty easy to show up, be seen, then slip away for a few minutes, off Sydney, and slip back before anyone noticed he was gone.

Though as we left Nickel City, I had to admit he didn't seem like he had much of a motive, either. Which I voiced to Sam and Chase in the parking lot.

"True," Sam agreed. "But if he's telling the truth, it opens up motive for someone else."

Chase raised a questioning eyebrow at her. "Jenni?"

She nodded. "Connor says Jenni didn't know about his plan to get back together with Sydney, but what if she found out—"

"And decided to take Sydney out of the picture?" I finished for her. It was certainly a possibility.

One I fully intended to explore when I saw Jenni at school tomorrow.

* * *

When I got home, Mom was, predictably, sitting in front of the computer. Only this time she wasn't wearing the intent frown of someone trying to figure out a dating site. She was smiling. And giggling. And blushing.

I was scared.

"Hey, Mom," I said tentatively.

Mom's head whipped up and instant guilt spread across her cheeks in a bright pink stain.

Uh-oh.

"Hartley. I didn't hear you come in."

"Whatcha doin'?" I asked, coming around the kitchen table to see her screen.

But before I could catch a glimpse of anything, she quickly closed the laptop.

"Nothing."

"It looked like you were doing something."

"Just typing."

"Typing what?"

"You're a nosy little one today, aren't you?"

I put my hands on my hips, doing the best imitation I could of her stern face, the one she always pulled out when it was time to clean my room. "Mom . . ."

She grinned and threw her hands up in a mock surrender gesture. "Okay, fine. If you must know, Miss Nosy, I was IM'ing with someone."

I scrunched up my nose. "Since when do you know

how to IM?" I asked.

"Ha-ha. Very funny, Hart."

"Okay, maybe a better question is who were you IM'ing with?" I asked.

"Not that it's any of your business," she answered, "but a man."

I knew I was going to regret this but . . .

"A man from Match dot com?"

She nodded. "Yes."

"Oh God, please tell me it's not Mr. Candlelit Dinners."

"Hartley!" she said, swatting me. "There's nothing wrong with a man being a romantic."

"Right," I said. "Long walks on the beach are totally cool. If your name is Fabio."

Mom swatted me again. "It's not him, okay? It's . . . someone else."

"Someone else, who? Can I see his profile?" I asked, reaching for her laptop lid.

But Mom quickly put her hand on top of it. "No."

I raised an eyebrow her way.

"I mean . . . it's private. This is a private conversation."

"Ew. You're not, like, sending dirty messages or anything, are you?"

Mom rolled her eyes at me. "We're having a perfectly normal adult conversation."

"'Adult' as in 'R-rated'?"

"Hartley . . ." Mom warned.

My turn to put my hands up. "Okay, okay. I'm just trying to look out for you, you know. There are a lot of perverts online."

She shot me a look. "He's not a pervert. And besides, we're just talking."

"That's how it starts. . . ."

"Hartley!"

"I'm just saying, that's all!"

"Look, don't you have some homework to do?" Mom said, making a shooing motion with her hands.

"It's Sunday."

"Then don't you have some friends to Facebook with?"

"I'm not sure 'Facebook' is a verb."

"Hart . . ." That warning tone crept into her voice again.

I nodded. "Okay. Fine. But don't say I didn't warn you when Mr. CyberLove starts sexting you!"

"Hartley!"

"I'm going," I said, backing out of the kitchen. As I hit the stairs, I heard the distinct sound of the laptop opening and fingers clicking on the keyboard again.

Yep. I was definitely scared.

ELEVEN

I SPENT THE REST OF THE DAY DOING MORE STUDYING FOR our upcoming AG midterm, more theorizing that went nowhere, and typing up my story for Monday's edition of the *Homepage*, as scant as it was. I pursed my lips, reading back through the copy. There was nothing here that was new: mostly just a vague recapping of Sydney's death, along with Mr. Tipkins's remarks from our interview on the cheating scandal. I had to turn in something to fill space in this week's edition, but it was fluff and I knew it.

I reluctantly emailed it to Chase just under the evening deadline, cringing as I waited for his reply.

It finally came in the form of a Facebook IM as I was tending my FarmVille plot that night, laptop on my legs while I lay back on my bed, digesting the last of Mom's gluten-free corn spaghetti with texturized vegetable protein balls.

got ur article, it said.

I paused, ready to defend its contents.

u happy with it? he asked.

I bit my lip. But any defense I had fell flat on my own ears, so instead of faking it, I told the truth.

it was fluff.

grin, he typed back.

i'll have something better soon. i swear!

i know.

Something about his confidence in me suddenly made the TVP balls in my stomach roll over one another. Especially since the faith was totally misplaced. Truth was, I had a lot of theories, but no real evidence that pointed to anyone as the Twittercidal maniac that had killed Sydney. And I was at a total dead end when it came to how Nicky had gotten those test answers, or if the two were even connected.

Which is why I was glad when Chase changed the subject.

hey . . . got plans 2morrow nite?

Okay, I was glad for about half a second. Then those TVP balls started moving again in nervous circles as I typed back, no. y?

meet me @ pizza my <3 4 dinner? 6?

For a full five seconds my entire body froze. My heart stopped, my lungs forgot how to breathe, and my fingers hovered stupidly over my keyboard. It sorta sounded like he was asking me out. But it had sorta sounded like that before with the football game. But this sounded more like it. Sorta.

u there?

yes, I typed back quickly.

yes ur there or yes 2 pizza?

I paused, my heart suddenly going from frozen to racing at a hundred miles a minute. And while I still wasn't sure what this all meant, somehow I found my fingers typing back the word both.

Cool, Chase responded. c u then.

Then he logged off, his icon disappearing.

I stared at the screen trying to process what had just happened.

I thought I had a date with Chase.

"I think I have a date with Chase tonight," I concluded the next morning as Sam and I stood outside Señorita Gonzalez's classroom waiting for Jenni Pritchard. (I'd found out last night from Erin Carter that Jessica Hanson said Cody Banks said that he had Spanish with Jenni first period. I only hoped my sources were correct.)

"No way!" Sam said, smacking me in the arm. "Deets."

I complied, relaying the IM conversation I'd had last night. When I was done, Sam was grinning so wide I could see her molars.

"Holy fermenting fish sticks! He's totally into you. I knew it!"

My stomach did that rolling thing again, only this time all it had to churn over was the breakfast latte I'd stopped for at Starbucks on the way to school.

"So," Sam asked, leaning in. "Are you into him?"

I bit my lip. "I don't know. Maybe. Sorta. We're friends, I guess."

"You guys would make such a cute couple," she said, staring off into space at a bank of lockers to our right. "You know what? I totally have some yarn leftover. I could make you matching heart bracelets!"

"Look, isn't that Jenni?" I asked, pointing to a brunette down the hallway, infinitely glad to be saved from that disturbing thought.

Jenni Pritchard had dark hair, dark eyes, and a tan complexion that had nothing to do with her ethnicity and everything to do with the tanning salon on North Santa Cruz Avenue. As usual, her hair was teased up a good four inches off her head, giving her five-foot frame a much needed boost in height. She was wearing short shorts, tall boots, and a chunky necklace with a lot of fake rhinestones in it. A wad of gum popped between her teeth as her head bobbed back and forth to a song in her earbuds.

I waved as she approached. "Jenni?" I called out.

She looked up, blinked, and frowned at me as her little

brain worked overtime to forage for recognition.

"Hartley Featherstone," I supplied. "I'm on the school paper."

She pulled one earbud out of her right ear. "Huh?"

"Um, Hartley Featherstone," I said again.

"Oh. 'Kay?" she said, more of a question than a statement.

"Can I talk to you for a minute?"

"Um, I guess," she said, popping her gum. "Why?"

"I wanted to ask you a couple questions for a story I'm doing for the school paper."

She blinked at me. "We have a school paper?"

I barely resisted the urge to roll my eyes.

"Yeah, we do. So, can I ask you a couple questions?"

"What kind of questions?"

"About Sydney Sanders's death."

"She committed suicide, right?"

"Actually, we think it might have been Twittercide," Sam said.

Jenni gave her a blank look.

"We think Sydney might have been killed while tweeting," I explained.

"No way! What a total dramathon that would be, right?"

"Right," I agreed. "Did you know that your boyfriend was going out with Sydney?"

Jenni looked from Sam to me. "Well, yeah, but that was totally in the past. Like . . . last week."

A whole week. It was getting harder and harder to resist that eye roll.

"Did you know Sydney?" I asked.

She shrugged. "Not well. I mean, I knew who she was, but we weren't, like, friends or anything, ya know?"

"What about Connor?" Sam jumped in. "How well did you know him before you guys got together?"

She shot Sam a blank look. "What's to know? He's hot."

One could resist only so long. My eyes did a three-sixty.

"So hot you dumped Ben Fisher for him?" Sam asked.

She shrugged her shoulders, her top's spaghetti straps coming *this* close to falling off. "Yeah. So?"

"After Connor dumped Sydney for you," I said.

"After she was kicked off the homecoming ballot," Sam added.

Jenni shrugged again. "So? She totally brought that on herself. Cheating is, like, way not cool, ya know?"

I formulated my next question carefully. While I didn't necessarily owe any vow of secrecy to Connor, I didn't really want to be the one to let his plan out of the bag.

"You weren't afraid that maybe Connor was only dating you to get the homecoming nomination?"

Jenni blinked at me again, popping her gum.

"Or that he might go back to Sydney after he won?"

"Why would he?" she asked.

Either she was ignorant of Connor's intentions or really good at playing dumb.

"I gotta ask," Sam said, cutting in. "What do you see in that guy?"

"Who, Connor? You're kidding, right? He's gorgeous."

"He certainly seems to think so," Sam mumbled.

"What?" Jenni asked, leaning in.

"Nothing."

"Back to Ben," I cut in. "You were seeing him before Connor?"

Jenni nodded. "That's right. But when Connor asked if I wanted to go out, I totally gave Ben the boot."

"Why?"

Again she blinked at me as if I was asking the most obvious questions in the world. "Um, Ben is a linebacker and Connor is a quarterback. Duh!"

Did her depth have no bounds?

"Where were you when Sydney died?" I asked.

"I dunno. What time was that?"

"Just after three."

She pursed her eyebrows together, scrunching up her nose as if thinking that hard really hurt. "Um, pro'ly shopping. I didn't have any shoes to go with the color corsage Connor was getting me. So I was at the mall every day last week after school."

Hardly an ironclad alibi, but the more time I spent chatting with Jenni, the less sure I was that she could carry out a plan to tie her shoes, much less kill someone. While shoving someone in a pool might not take a PhD, covering your tracks afterward did. I'd venture to say that if Jenni had been the one to off Sydney, her teased DNA would have been all over the crime scene.

"Lookit," Jenni said, popping one hip out. "If you really think someone killed Sydney, I'd take a look at that so-called best friend of hers."

I raised an eyebrow. "So-called? Why do you say that?"

"Because Quinn hooked up with Connor before he dumped Sydney."

"O. M. G," Sam said. "She did not!"

Jenni smirked. "Oh, yes she did. Right before Connor and I got together. He told me he was studying after school with Quinn and Sydney one day, and Sydney had to leave for yearbook committee. The second she was gone, Quinn was all over him. She totally made out with him."

I refrained from pointing out that it took two to tongue tango, instead asking, "Did Sydney find out about it?"

Jenni shrugged. "I dunno. But it might explain why she ratted Quinn out to the vice principal."

Good point. It also might explain why Quinn had seemed like she was hiding something when she'd talked to us. I wondered what else she might have been hiding . . . like the fact she'd Twittercided her best friend? (I had to admit, Sam's new word was growing on me.)

"Why would Connor tell you this?" Sam asked.

Oh, good question. I leaned in to hear the answer.

"Quinn wouldn't leave him alone," Jenni said. "At first I thought there was something going on there, like Connor was totally cheating on me or something, but then Connor told me what had happened. I mean, she was texting him, like, all the time. Like, she seriously thought he might be into her."

"And you're sure he wasn't?" I asked.

"Puh-lease. Quinn Leslie is not even close to homecoming queen material. Once Connor told me what happened, I was so not worried about her."

But had Sydney been worried about her? Or, more important, had Quinn been worried about Sydney? It was hard to imagine someone killing over a narcissist like Connor, but I guess stranger things had happened.

As I contemplated this new bit of information, the bell rang, echoing off the pea-green hallway walls.

Jenni stuck her other earbud back in, effectively ending the interview, and ducked into Spanish. Sam took off for her AP statistics class, promising to meet me at lunch in the cafeteria, and I hoofed it to lit, still mulling over what Jenni had said.

If it was true that Quinn had made out with Sydney's

boyfriend, that put a whole new spin on their friendship. And if Sydney had retaliated by getting Quinn busted for cheating, maybe Quinn had upped the ante in her revenge and killed Sydney. One thing was certain: I had to talk to Quinn again.

I spent first period in a haze, barely paying attention to Shakespeare's sonnets as I watched the clock tick down with agonizing slowness. Ditto PE and American Government, where I could have sworn the clock's hands stood still the entire time Mr. Bleaker explained the Articles of the Confederation in excruciating detail. By the time I finally got out of fourth-period Spanish, I fairly raced for the cafeteria. Unfortunately, my sprint carried me right past the teachers' lounge, and as the door opened, Mr. Tipkins emerged, a cup of coffee in one hand and a stack of papers in the other.

"Hartley," he said, hailing me. "I was actually hoping I'd run into you."

"You were?" I asked, wracking my brain to make sure I hadn't said anything bad about him in the article that had run in that morning's *Homepage*. "Um . . . why?"

"I saw the article in this morning's paper."

"Uh . . . you did?" I hedged.

He nodded. "It looks like you're doing a very thorough job of investigating where Sydney got those test answers."

I did a mental sigh of relief. "Thanks. I'm certainly trying."

"Have you turned up any new information about how they got out?"

I bit my lip. "Not really." Which was mostly true. While I knew Nicky was involved, I still didn't know who had given Nicky the answers, so technically I didn't know how his cheats had gotten out. Just where they went once they did.

And, as Nicky had pointed out, I had no proof.

"Well, I'd like to be kept in the loop on this," Mr. Tipkins said.

I nodded. "Sure," I said. "No prob."

"I take the security of my tests very seriously," he added.

"I understand," I said, backing away. "Trust me— when I find out how those answers got out, you'll be the first to know!" I quickly turned and continued my sprint all the way to the cafeteria.

By the time I got there, Quinn, fresh off her suspension, was already at a table near the back with half the lacrosse team, a tray of Monday Meat(ish)loaf in front of her.

I quickly approached, ignoring the way my own stomach growled at the scent of food. (Even if it was only food-ish.)

Quinn looked up, conversation around her hushing as

someone clearly not of the Sporty Girl ranks came near.

"What?" Quinn asked. A less-than-friendly greeting, but then again, I had a less-than-friendly question to ask her.

"I have some new info about Sydney," I told her.

At the mention of Sydney's name, all eyes hit the floor, a mix of sadness and awkward emotions filling the air. I saw that several of the girls were wearing black mourning bands on their arms, Quinn included.

"I'd like to talk to you about her," I pressed Quinn.

"So talk," she challenged me.

I glanced at the row of girls in matching ponytails and sweats seated next to her, all eyes trying desperately to avoid mine.

"I think maybe we should talk in private."

A couple of the other girls exchanged glances, but something in my tone must have convinced Quinn, as she just shrugged and pushed away from the table and led the way to an empty table in the corner. She leaned against the end and crossed her arms over her chest, defensive before I could even begin. "Okay, what's so private?"

Since she seemed to be a fan of the direct, I dove right in.

"You made out with Connor while he and Sydney were still going out."

Fire instantly lit up Quinn's eyes as she narrowed them at me. "Who told you that?"

I gulped. "Um . . . a source. Is it true?"

She pursed her lips, and I could tell a lie was just on the tip of her tongue.

But not knowing who my source was, she didn't know what kind of proof (or lack thereof) I had. So she bit the inside of her cheeks and finally decided on, "So what?" She stuck her chin out defiantly.

"Did Sydney know?"

Quinn paused, seemingly genuine emotion suddenly welling in her eyes. "Yeah. She found out."

"How?"

"She saw a text I'd sent Connor on his phone and called me out on it. So I told her the truth. Connor was into me."

Huh. That wasn't exactly how Jenni had described it, but I wasn't going to be the one to burst Quinn's bubble.

"I can't imagine Sydney was very happy about that," I prodded.

Quinn shook her head. "No. She was pissed. Not that I can blame her. She'd just found out her boyfriend was leaving her for me."

"He told you that?" I asked, unable to keep the disbelief out of my voice.

"Well, no," she admitted. "But I could see it coming."

I wasn't sure who I felt more sorry for, Dead Sydney or Clueless Quinn.

"So, let me guess," I said. "To get back at you, Sydney

told the principal that you were involved in the cheating."

Quinn nodded. "Which was totally not cool. But, like I said, I don't blame her for being angry."

"But then Connor started dating Jenni, not you."

Quinn squared her jaw. "It's just because Jenni is up for homecoming court."

"So after the homecoming dance . . ." I trailed off.

"He's dumping her and getting together with me."

Oh boy. Was Quinn ever in for a rude awakening.

"Okay, let's play 'let's pretend' for a moment, shall we?" I said.

Quinn stuck her chin out again but didn't stop me, so I plowed on.

"Let's pretend that Sydney hadn't been killed. And Connor was, as you said, only with Jenni for the homecoming vote. What if, after it was over, he was going to go back to Sydney and not you?"

Quinn blinked at me. "No. He was going to get together with me."

Either she really believed that or someone had been taking after-school drama classes. "I hate to break it to you," I said, "but that's not what Connor told me. He said he was going back to Sydney."

Quinn shook her head. "That's not possible. He's into me. He made out with me on his own bed. Guys don't do that unless they're into you."

I bit my lip. I hated to tell her but some guys just made out with you to make out with you. Being into you wasn't a given.

Quinn was still shaking her head. "You know what? It doesn't matter. Sydney's gone, so clearly Connor has one choice left."

I gave her a hard look, hunkering my eyebrows down over my eyes. "Right. Now that Sydney's gone."

"Wait—what's with the eyebrows?" she said. "What are you trying to say?"

"Did you kill Sydney to clear the field to Connor?" I asked point-blank.

Quinn's eyes went big. "Me? No. God, no! She killed herself. Over the guilt from ratting me out to the VP."

"I thought you said overachievers didn't kill themselves," I pointed out, repeating what she'd told me in our first interview.

Quinn shrugged. "Well, I've had some time to think about it. And I think she did. I mean, I was her best friend. She must have felt really bad about what she did. Look, are we done? Because we only have fifteen minutes left of lunch and I gotta eat."

While I would have liked to grill her further, I honestly didn't know what else to ask. Plus, I intended to stuff as much meat-ish loaf into my own mouth in fifteen minutes as I could.

So I watched Quinn walk away, then grabbed a tray

and contemplated what she'd told me as I wolfed down my lunch.

Everyone seemed to have a different theory for why Sydney had killed herself. Guilt, depression, or, as Raley thought, teen statistic. I had to admit, Sydney's life had been a bit of a mess. But even so, I kept going back to the fact that people who kill themselves usually do it after the secret meeting they've set up, not before. If Sydney really had committed suicide, why not wait until after meeting with me? It just didn't make any sense.

Unfortunately, by the time I was dumping my tray and heading to sixth period, I was no closer to an answer. I was just pulling my chem book out of my bag when my phone buzzed in my pocket.

I looked down at the readout.

It was Nicky Williams. I raised an eyebrow. He was the last person I'd expected to hear from.

"Nicky?" I answered, leaning against a bank of lockers outside Mrs. Perry's classroom.

"Hey. I need to talk to you."

"Okay. Talk away."

"No." I could hear him shaking his head. "In person. They may be listening in."

"They?" I asked.

"The cops. Look, one of them came to see me after you did yesterday. He said I was obstructing justice, hampering an investigation, all kinds of legal stuff like that."

Raley. I wondered what the chances were he'd found Nicky out on his own and not by following me to the mall.

"Anyway," Nicky went on, "I'm ready to talk. I'll tell you everything you want to know about the test answers as long as you keep my name out of it. Once it's printed in the paper, the cops will leave me alone, right?"

I shrugged. It was possible.

"Where can we meet?" I asked. "Are you at school?"

Again I could hear rustling as Nicky's head shook back and forth in the negative. "No. School's too dangerous. Someone might see us. Tonight. Meet me at Oak Meadow Park. Eight p.m. By the train."

"Okay," I agreed. I knew the park well. It was on Blossom Hill Road just down from the junior high we'd all gone to, and not only completely deserted after sunset but completely dark. Usually not a combo I was a big fan of, but I was willing to go just about anywhere to get this story. Which was exactly what I promised Nicky.

"Eight p.m. Oak Meadow. I'll be there."

TWELVE

THE REST OF THE DAY WENT BY IN A BLUR OF HOMEWORK assignments, boring lectures, and one pop quiz in trig. And as much as Sydney's Twittercide was on my mind, another event was slowly pushing its way to the forefront: my date with Chase.

I still wasn't entirely sure how I felt about it. Chase was nothing like the guys I'd gone out with before. Cole Perkins was my first real boyfriend. We'd gone out freshman year, but things had fizzled when Cole decided my making out with him in his bedroom when his parents were out of town meant we were soul mates. And I'd decided I wanted a soul mate that didn't kiss like a golden retriever. After Cole I'd dated Josh DuPont who, while scoring a ten on the hot-o-meter, had ended up cheating on me with the president of the Chastity Club and dragging me headfirst into a murder investigation, after which he'd switched schools to avoid the gossip mill and hadn't been seen since. To say I didn't have great luck in the guy department was like saying Ryan Seacrest didn't have great luck in the height department: total understatement.

A fact that left me with an uneasy feeling in my stomach about having pizza with Chase. Chase and I were so different that it had honestly taken me some time before I'd come to see him as a genuine friend. Putting him into the role of something more than a friend suddenly sounded like dangerous territory. Territory that left a weird sensation running through my stomach. Nervous. Anxious. Kinda like I'd eaten a bad Tuesday Taco.

Sam had to meet with her SAT tutor again after school, but as soon as she was done, she came straight to my house.

"Whoa," she said, walking into my room. "What happened?"

I looked around. Clothes littered every surface, jeans mixing with skirts mixing with capris, and T-shirts, and sweaters, and boots, and me in the middle of it all, trying on my tenth outfit since school had let out.

"I need to be casual but not too casual. Dressy but not too dressy. I need him to think I just threw on the first thing I found and that I'm not taking this too seriously or overthinking it or even that I was thinking about it at all. Because I'm not. I'm totally not thinking about him, and

I don't want him to think I was thinking about him, but I don't want him to think that I'm not thinking about him, because clearly he thought about me enough to ask me out and it would be mean not to be thinking about him at all, so I need just the right amount of thinking, and I'm not sure if that means boots and a skirt or skinny jeans and ballet flats. Help!"

I paused and took a deep breath, realizing I'd forgotten the importance of oxygen during my plea.

"Okay." Sam walked in and put her book bag down on the bed. She stood in front of me, doing a slow up and down with her eyes. "I think we can fix this. First thing's first. Your hair."

"Hair?" I squeaked out. "Oh, fluffin' fudge. I didn't even think about hair!"

Two hours later I'd done the one thing I'd sworn I would never do again—let Sam dress me to go out. Though I had to admit as I checked out the results in the full-length mirror on my closet door I might not have been wrong in doing so. She'd advised on a mid-thigh white denim skirt over a pair of gray leggings. She'd paired that with a long, lean gray tee with rhinestones at the neckline and a lightweight, three-quarter sleeve cardigan. And, while I was a respectable B cup, the push-up bra Sam had insisted on made my boobs stand at attention, giving me cleavage to rival that of any member of the cheer squad.

On my feet were a pair of silver three-inch heels that I could almost walk in without wobbling, which Sam had pulled from her own closet. Overall, I had to admit I looked pretty dang hot.

A thought I held on to with a two-fisted grip as I walked the mile from my house to the Pizza My Heart downtown, that taco feeling churning in my gut with every step.

By the time I finally hit the pizza place, I could feel blisters forming on my heels, and my feet were sweating so badly that I feared the effect of my hotness would be overshadowed by my need for Odor-Eaters.

I paused outside the restaurant. Pushed a couple stray strands of hair off my face. Did a quick breath check. Tried to remember how confident I'd looked in my bedroom mirror. Then pushed through the doors of Pizza My Heart at exactly six o'clock for my dinner with Chase.

The place wasn't huge, and I spotted him right away. He was standing at a table in the back of the restaurant. His back was to me, but his spiky hair was unmistakable. It was mussed into a softer look than usual, kind of tousled like he'd been out in the wind for a while. He wore a black T-shirt, jeans that were somewhere perfectly in the middle of tight and low slung, clinging just enough to hold on to his hips but not so tight that he looked like a cast member of *Glee*. Black workboots ended the outfit, and a silver chain hung from his pocket.

I did another deep breath thing as I approached.

"Hey," I said, tapping him on the shoulder.

He spun around.

Then his mouth dropped open just a little as he took in Sam's handiwork, his eyes honing in on the result of her push-up.

"Heeeeeey," he said slowly. "Wow, you look—"

"Hot!" another voice finished.

I whipped my head to the left and saw Ashley Stannic sitting at Chase's table.

What the . . . ?

"Nice shoes," Ashley said. "You going out later?"

I blinked at her. "I, uh . . ." Slowly I let my gaze shift around the table and realized not only was Ashley crashing my dinner with Chase, but Chris Fret was sitting at the table as well, along with a guy I recognized from Spanish class.

Chase cleared his throat beside me. "I, uh, I'm glad you could make it, Hartley."

"Thanks," I answered, hoping the confusion rattling around in my brain wasn't clear in my voice.

"So, now that we're all here," he said, turning back to the table at large. "The reason I invited everyone out for pizza was to introduce you all to the newest member of the *Homepage* staff."

I froze.

He invited everyone.

I suddenly felt like the word *moron* was stamped across my forehead. Chase hadn't asked me out. He'd asked one of his reporters out. I silently prayed the floor would open up and swallow me whole as I only halfway listened to Chase, embarrassment all but drowning him out as it pounded in my overheated ears.

"Guys, this is Mike Watson," Chase said, gesturing to Spanish Class Guy. "He's going to be covering all the away games for *HHH*, as it's come to my attention that Chris may be a bit overworked."

Chris grinned sheepishly at the veiled reference to his cheating attempt.

"Great to have you," Ashley said. Chris mumbled something similar. Chase clapped Mike on the back.

All I could do was stare dumbly.

Somehow, I managed to sit, congratulate Mike, and even stuff half a slice of pepperoni pizza into my mouth, even though all I wanted to do was crawl into that big black hole. I was so stupid. I was the queen of Stupidville. The Duchess of Moronland. The Empress of Misunderstandingtown.

And by the way Chase kept sending sidelong glances at my rhinestone-framed cleavage and spiky heels, I had a bad feeling he knew it. Clearly I was overdressed for pizza with friends. Clearly I had taken some pains to change after school. Clearly I was expecting something way more exciting than a new sports guy.

Clearly I needed to have my head examined.

By seven, I couldn't take it anymore. I mumbled something about a previous commitment and slipped from the table as Ashley laid out her ideas for this weekend's coverage of the homecoming dance. Chase moved to get up as I slipped from the table, but I stopped him with a quick, "See you at school," over my shoulder as I ran (or tried to—the heels were really wobbly) for the door.

I took half an hour to indulge in a pity-party chocolate bar from Powell's before I hoofed it down North Santa Cruz Ave to meet Nicky at Oak Meadow Park. I was determined that despite my detour into the stupid lane, my night was not going to be a total bust. So Chase only saw me as a reporter. Fine. That was easier on my stomach anyway. But this week I'd better be a fudging good one and turn in something more than fluff.

I walked as fast as my legs would take me in the tight skirt and ridiculously high heels that Sam had made me wear, all the while chanting to myself that I would never listen to her wardrobe advice again.

I looked down at my cell readout as I crossed Highway 9—7:54. I picked up the pace, half jogging until my calves cramped up, then checked my cell again. 7:58. No way was

I going to make our rendezvous time. I bit my lip, praying that Nicky would wait for me.

At 8:06 I finally hit the corner of University and the gates to Oak Meadow Park.

As far as city parks went, it was large: a playground with two big jungle gyms at one end and a carousel and miniature train station at the other. Between them spanned picnic areas and a large expanse of grass used by the local soccer league in the summer.

At this time of night, everything was dark and the gates were closed. I did a brief over-the-shoulder, waiting until there was a break in the passing traffic, then quickly hopped the fence. Or, it would have been quickly if my stupid heels hadn't gotten stuck in the metal diamonds. I finally kicked them off and threw them over the gate, cringing as they skidded in the dirt on the other side. Sam wasn't going to be happy about that. On the second try, I slipped over the fence, landed with a thud on the other side, put the shoes back on (only scuffed a little), then picked my way down the gravel pathway to the miniature train station.

The train was a big draw for kids during the weekends and summer break, the station packed with lines of toddlers waiting for the three-dollar rides. But tonight the train was silent, and the giant clock set in the Victorian-style steeple of the station ticked eerily in the dark.

I wrapped my arms around myself, wishing I'd worn something a little warmer, and quickly made tracks toward the quiet station.

I was a few feet away when I spotted a figure in the shadows, just behind the roundhouse. By the dark hair sticking out from under a skater beanie, I could tell it was Nicky. I was about to call out when I saw another person approach him.

I paused. Nicky hadn't said anything about bringing friends. Suddenly I felt a little outnumbered, standing in the shadows.

Which was ridiculous, because I was just going to talk and get a story. The dark, the quiet, and the eerie Victorian station were giving me the creeps.

At least that's what I told myself as I approached the two figures. Only they weren't paying any attention to me. They were talking to each other. Loudly. Arguing, I realized as I got closer. I was too far away to hear what they were actually saying, but the second figure started flapping his (her? It was too dark to tell) arms at Nicky. Nicky stepped back, his voice raised, though the only words I caught were, "Dude, no!"

I paused, not sure I wanted to get in the middle of this, whatever this was. I could see Figure Two was dressed in dark pants and a dark Windbreaker. He (she?) was close to Nicky's height, but that was all I could make out. Male, female, old, young were all swallowed up by the darkness.

But I could see Nicky was getting more and more agitated. He shook his head, waved his arms. Finally he shouted, "It's over!" loudly enough to make Figure Two stop in his-slash-her tracks. Nicky turned his back on the guy, as if to emphasize the over-ness of their situation, and started walking away.

I opened my mouth to call out to him.

But that's when I saw it.

Figure Two bent over and picked up a rock that was lying at his feet. From the effort it took him to stand back up again, I could tell it was heavy. I watched in horror as he took a step toward Nicky, lifted the rock above his body, and brought it down with a thud on the back of Nicky's head.

Nicky made a pathetic sort of grunt, then slumped forward, crumpling to the ground.

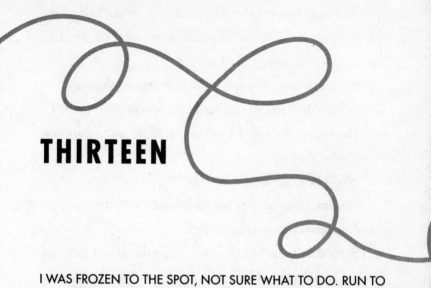

THIRTEEN

I WAS FROZEN TO THE SPOT, NOT SURE WHAT TO DO. RUN TO Nicky's aid? Make a citizen's arrest of Figure Two? Call for help?

Being that there were a lot more rocks lying around for Figure Two's convenience, I decided on option three and pulled my cell from my pocket. I backtracked toward the street as I dialed 911, all the while keeping one eye on Nicky's prone form.

Which meant I wasn't watching where I was walking, which meant I tripped over a stick on the ground and stumbled to catch my balance.

Figure Two's head snapped up.

Oh, fluffin' fudge.

I turned and ran blindly through the trees toward the road again, phone to my ear, though I was only halfway listening to it ring on the other end. The other half of me was completely engrossed in panic. After what seemed like an eternity, someone picked up.

"Nine-one-one. What is your emergency, please?"

"I *(pant)* just *(pant)* saw someone killed! *(pant, pant)*"

"I'm sorry, ma'am. I can't understand you. Can you please slow down?"

"No! The killer heard me trip!"

"Ma'am, can you give me your location?" the operator asked, her voice annoyingly calm.

I paused as I reached the gate again, the bright lights of passing cars on the other side a small comfort. I sucked in a large gulp of chilled air and stopped to catch my breath, listening behind me for any sound of footsteps.

I heard nothing but my own Doberman-esque breathing.

"I'm at Oak Meadow Park at the corner of University and Blossom Hill," I told the dispatcher.

"I'm sending someone out to your location now. Please stay on the line with me until they get there."

"Okay," I whimpered. "But hurry. I think they killed Nicky."

"Don't worry. Help is on the way," she said. And even though I knew there was nothing she could do from the other end of a phone call, her voice did make me feel a little less alone.

I managed to hop back over the gate to the street side,

and sat down on the curb to wait for help, one ear listening for any sign of the killer, one listening to the dispatcher who continued talking in smooth, even tones.

After ten cold minutes, my butt was numb, goose bumps were permanently embedded in my arms, and the red and blue lights of a police cruiser pulled down Blossom Hill. I jumped up and waved my arms madly at the guy behind the wheel, who pulled to a stop in front of me.

I'd never been so relieved to see law enforcement in my life.

After I explained what I'd seen, the cop grabbed a flashlight from the front seat and disappeared into the park.

I waited alone on the sidewalk again. I was just starting to worry that maybe Figure Two had done the officer in, too, when an ambulance pulled to a stop at the curb behind the police cruiser.

Two paramedics got out, then grabbed a stretcher from the back. One of the guys pulled a pair of wire cutters from the back of the van, making short work of the locked gate, then they wheeled the stretcher down to the field.

Stretcher not body bag.

Did that mean that Nicky was still alive? That he was okay? That maybe I'd just watched an assault and not a murder?

I hugged my arms around myself, anxiously waiting

for that stretcher to come back. While Nicky was a cheater and a liar and had basically threatened my best friend, I still found myself quietly chanting, "Please be alive, please be alive," as I shifted from foot to foot on the sidewalk.

A couple minutes later, the officer climbed back up the hill, his form bobbing through the trees as he approached me.

"Is he dead?" I asked.

The officer shook his head, and I felt myself sag with relief.

"He's hurt. How badly, it's hard to tell right now. But the paramedics are doing all they can."

All they can. That wasn't the most positive phrase. I was about to ask more when another car came around the corner, lights flashing red and blue. Apparently in addition to paramedics, my officer had called for backup. Unfortunately, as the car pulled to a stop at the curb, I recognized that backup.

Tall, red-haired, round-bellied. And the one thing that could make my night worse.

Detective Raley.

I briefly contemplated running again, but since blisters were already bruising my heels, I nixed that idea, instead drawing myself up as tall as I could while he approached.

"Hartley," he said.

"Detective Raley."

He took a deep breath, staring off into the tree line. "Why is it that whenever anything criminal goes on in this town, there you are?"

"Great reporter's instinct?"

He shot me a look. Clearly his opinion differed on that one.

"All right, let's hear it," he said, pulling a notebook and pen from his back pocket. "What were you doing here?"

I pursed my lips together, not sure how much to tell him. Best-case scenario: Nicky was unconscious and certainly not talking to me tonight. Worst case: He was never talking to anyone again.

"I was meeting Nicky," I finally confessed.

"Why?" he asked, bushy eyebrows frowning.

"I was interviewing him for the school paper."

"About what?"

"Stuff."

"What kind of stuff?"

"School stuff."

"Can you be more specific?"

"Yes."

He gave me an expectant look. "Well?"

"Oh, did you mean, 'will I be more specific'? Because 'can' implies an ability. I have the ability to be more specific, but if you're asking if I have the intention of complying with a request to be more specific, then what you really mean is 'will I be more specific.'"

I watched Raley grind his back teeth together, his nostrils flaring. If I'd had to guess, he was employing some sort of anger management technique and mentally counting to ten.

"Okay, will you please be more specific, Hartley?" he asked, his teeth still cemented together in a grimace.

"Sure. What was the question?"

A vein bulged in Raley's forehead, and I was pretty sure he was one blood-pressure point away from a full-blown aneurysm.

"Did you see who hit Nicky?" he asked instead, changing gears.

"Kinda."

"Christ," he muttered under his breath. "What does 'kinda' mean?"

"It means I saw someone hit him on the head, but I couldn't see who did the hitting. It was really dark and the guy was keeping to the shadows."

"Guy?" Raley asked, jumping on the word. "So it was a male you saw?"

I bit my lip. "Honestly? I'm not sure. Maybe."

Raley sighed, flipping his notebook shut. "So you didn't really see anything?"

I bit my lip. "Sorry," I said, sincerely meaning it. Maybe if I had gotten a good look, we'd both have our killer now.

"Okay," Raley said, resigned to my status as the worst witness ever. "I'll have someone drive you home."

Considering the blisters were growing to astronomical proportions, I got in the car. (Besides, it wasn't like he gave me much choice.)

The first uniformed officer drove me home in silence, though the second he walked me to the front door, it was clear someone had called ahead to Mom.

"Oh, Hartley!" She tackled me in the foyer, grabbing me in a hug so tight I felt it rearranging my internal organs.

But honestly? After the night I'd had, I needed a spleen-displacing hug. I wrapped my arms around her middle and hugged back. After a long comforting moment, Mom pulled back to look at me.

"Are you okay, honey?" she asked, her eyes searching my person for visible scars.

I nodded, putting on my bravest face.

"Oh, sweetie, don't cry," Mom said, hugging me again.

Okay, so my bravest wasn't all that brave at the moment.

I sniffled, getting myself under control as the uniformed officer gave Mom a quick rundown of what had happened. When he was done, Mom looked about as aneurysm-close as Raley had.

"God, Hartley, the park after dark? What were you thinking?"

Which was totally unfair. I mean, it's not like I knew I was going to witness a near murder. But, instead of arguing, I opted for the answer that would get me upstairs, in bed, and most important, out of these heels, the fastest.

"Sorry."

"A deserted park?"

"Sorry."

"You could have been killed!"

"Sorry."

"Is that all you have to say for yourself?"

I shrugged. "Super-duper sorry?"

Mom rolled her eyes. "It's late. Go upstairs. We'll talk about this tomorrow."

I nodded, gladly making my escape.

The next morning, true to her word, Mom cornered me before school, giving me a lecture on leaving the house after dark as she virtually force-fed me a plate of vegan bacon and I-Can't-Believe-It's-Not-Egg-Whites.

And, as if the SMother wasn't enough, by the time the first-period bell rang, I'd gotten two dozen texts asking if it was true that (A) Nicky was attacked in front of me (yes!), (B) I'd gotten Nicky attacked (no!), and (C) there would be a Sydney tribute before the homecoming game (which I'm pretty sure was sent to me by mistake, since Ashley was on the homecoming beat).

By lunch, everyone had heard the news about Nicky, but there was one person who I knew would have the real deets. The instant I reached the cafeteria, I zeroed in on Drea, who was taking her tray of Tuesday Tacos to a table near the back.

"Drea," I called, hailing her as I approached.

She looked up. Then shot me a death look. "You!" she yelled, pointing one finger my way.

I stopped dead in my tracks.

"Uh, me?"

"Because of you and your nosiness, Nicky's in the hospital."

Honestly? It was more because of Nicky's cheating-ness, but I decided this was not the time to point that out.

"Is he going to be okay?" I asked instead.

She sat down and popped the top on her chocolate milk. "Maybe. He has a skull fracture. And a concussion."

I cringed. "That sounds bad."

She nodded, her eyes turning red with the effort not to cry and ruin her mascara. "It is. He was unconscious for a long time, and now they're keeping him in the hospital for a couple days for observation. And I can't even see him," she said, a sob escaping.

"I'm sorry," I said, putting a hand on her arm. "Listen, Nicky was at the park last night because he had something to tell me. Something about the test answers. I think he was going to tell me where he got them. Did he say anything to you about it?"

Drea shrugged. "He said he was going to meet you, but he didn't say why."

"Did he tell you where he got the answers?"

She shook her head. "No. He said he couldn't. He didn't want to get me in trouble in case he ever got caught. He was protecting me," she said, breaking down in a sob again.

"Have you talked to Nicky since the attack?"

She nodded. "Once. But he's not supposed to be on the phone very long. He needs to rest."

"What did he say? Who attacked him?"

She shrugged. "He didn't tell me."

I pursed my lips together. "Look, Drea, this is a matter of life and death," I told her, not being entirely overdramatic. "I need to talk to Nicky and find out what he knows."

Drea pulled out her cell and scrolled through menus. "They're only letting family in to see him, but I can give you the number I have to call his room."

"Perfect." I grabbed my own cell, typing in the number as Drea recited it.

I thanked her and stepped outside before hitting Send.

Four rings in, a woman answered the phone.

"Hello?"

"Uh, hi. I wanted to speak to Nicky?"

"May I ask who is calling?"

"Hartley. We're friends from school," I said, stretching the truth just a little.

"I see. Well, this is Nicky's mom, and I'm sorry, Hartley, but Nicky isn't taking any calls right now. He's been through quite an ordeal and needs his rest. I'll tell him you called and that you're thinking of him."

"It's important!" I protested.

"Thank you for calling," she said. Then hung up.

But I wasn't giving up that easily.

I slipped back into the cafeteria, scanning the rows of tables for Sam. I finally spotted her near the center of the room, seated next to Kyle. They were feeding each other bites of taco shell from Sam's plate. Which in itself was cute enough to be slightly nauseating, but they had taken it over the top with their outfits today. Sam was wearing a pink T-shirt that said, "I like Boys," and Kyle was wearing a baby-blue one with the word "Boy" in the center.

I tried to ignore the oozing cuteness and made a beeline toward their table.

"Hey. I need your help," I said, plopping down next to Sam.

"Dude!" Kyle said. "Everyone's been tweeting about Nicky. Sucks."

I nodded. "Yeah, that's kinda what I need help with." I

quickly filled Sam and Kyle in on what had happened the night before.

"Someone clearly didn't want Nicky to talk to me," I finished.

"Just like they didn't want Sydney to talk to you," Sam pointed out.

"Whoa. Déjà vu, dude," Kyle said.

"Which is why we need to get to Nicky and fast," I agreed. "If he really was hit by the person behind stealing the test answers, chances are the guy—"

"Or girl," Sam put in.

"—will come back for him."

"So how are we going to do that?" Kyle asked. "Didn't you say his mom isn't letting him on the phone?"

I nodded. "We need to talk to him in person."

"How?" Sam asked.

I pursed my lips together. "We go to the hospital."

Sam shook her head. "But if his mom won't let Drea see Nicky, what makes you think she'll let us?"

"She won't," I agreed. "Which is why we need to sneak in. And that's where you come in."

It took a series of texts to Sam that spanned sixth and seventh periods to convince her that sneaking into a hospital room was not an offense that would go on her permanent record and ruin her chances at Stanford. By the time school got out, she was 90 percent on board with my plan, which was just enough to get her on the bus that ran down Los Gatos Boulevard to the hospital.

Fifteen minutes later, we were hiking our book bags onto our shoulders as we pushed into the lobby. Immediately we were assaulted with the smells of disinfectant, rubbing alcohol, and latex gloves. I swallowed down the unpleasant memories of booster shots and penicillin the scents conjured up and made my way toward the room number Drea had supplied.

After about four wrong turns, we found it. It was upstairs in the pediatric wing, at the end of a long hallway. Right in front of the nurses' station.

Sam and I casually walked past, peeking in the door. As I'd anticipated, standing vigil not only over the phone but over Nicky as well was a large woman with salt and pepper hair. I'd bet anything she was Nicky's mom.

"Okay, Sam, this is where you come in," I said. "I need a really good distraction."

She bit her lip. "Fine. But you so owe me one after this."

I nodded. "Tell you what—I'll forgive you for dressing me in those hecka-blisters heels."

She contemplated this for a moment. "Just be quick. I don't know how long I can keep Mom away."

With that, Sam turned away and strode purposefully toward the nurses' station. I watched her take a deep breath . . . then let it out on a sigh as she collapsed onto the floor.

Immediately the nurse behind the desk dove toward her, calling out to another nurse, the two of them quickly surrounding her.

As I'd hoped, Nicky's mom came out of the room to see what the commotion was.

It was now or never.

I quickly slipped down the hallway and into Nicky's room.

He was propped up in bed, a tray of Jell-O in front of him and a TV in the corner playing a SpongeBob episode. There was a bandage wrapped around his head, and I could see that his long hair had been shaved off on one side.

He looked up as I entered, blinking at me, confusion clear on his face as his concussed brain tried to figure out what I was doing there.

"Hartley?" he asked.

"Hey," I said, quickly going to his side, one eye on the door, where I expected his mom to bust back in at any second. "We need to talk, and I don't have much time."

"How did you get in here?" he asked, looking past me.

I shook my head. "Not important. What is important is that you tell me what you were going to tell me at the park."

Nicky bit the inside of his cheek. He looked down at his hands. "I don't remember."

He was the worst liar ever.

"What do you mean, you don't remember?" I asked, desperation kicking in.

He looked up at me again. "I got hit on the head. I don't remember."

"You're totally lying."

"Prove it," he said jutting his chin forward.

Since I couldn't, I changed tactics. "Who attacked you?"

He shrugged. "I got hit from behind. I didn't see anyone."

"But I saw you arguing with the person first! You must have seen his face then?"

He paused, something flitting across his eyes. If I'd had to guess, I'd say it was fear. "Sorry," he said. "I don't remember that."

"Look, if you're scared of this guy, the police can protect you. Just tell me what you know. Once it's out in the open, you'll be safe."

"Right." He snorted. "Last time I decided to tell you something I got my head bashed in and ended up here," he said, gesturing to the hospital room around him. "The only way I'm going to be safe is by keeping my big mouth shut."

"Nicky, please," I pleaded. Sam could only play sick for so long. Any second now, his mom would be back.

"I've said all I have to say." He clamped his mouth shut for emphasis.

"Nicky—"

But that's as far as I got, as Mom pushed through the doorway. Her eyes narrowed, clearly surprised to see me.

"Who are you?" she asked, her voice holding a sharp edge that said a call to security was about half a second away.

"Uh . . . I'm . . ."—I quickly grabbed a pillow from behind Nicky and fluffed it—"I'm a candy striper. Yeah, I volunteer here at the hospital. Just came in to make sure our patient is comfortable." I gave Mom a big toothy smile as I replaced Nick's fluffed pillow.

Nicky opened his mouth to speak, but I shot him a death look.

He clamped it shut again.

"Oh," Mom said, her posture relaxing. "In that case, do you have any magazines? I'd really love something to read in here."

"Absolutely," I lied. "No prob. One magazine coming up!" I ducked my head to avoid Mom reading the lie plainly written there.

Which was my fatal mistake.

I would have totally gotten away without anyone being the wiser if I'd just watched where I was going instead of plowing headfirst into someone else.

"Ohmigosh, I'm so sorry," I said, whipping my eyes up.

Straight to Detective Raley's.

FOURTEEN

"HARTLEY," RALEY SAID.

"HARTLEY," RALEY SAID.

I cleared my throat. "Uh, hi. We meet again, huh?" I commented, doing a poor attempt at humor.

Which, judging from the scowl on his face, was totally lost on him. He made a sound somewhere between a grunt and a snort and answered with a "What are you doing here?"

"I'm . . . uh . . ." I quickly looked around the nurses' station for any sign of Sam, but thankfully, my accomplice was long gone. "I'm . . . volunteering," I said, going with the same story I'd told Nicky's mom. It was almost the truth. I mean, I had offered to get Nicky's mom a magazine, right?

Raley narrowed his eyes. "Really?"

"Really."

"Since when do you volunteer at the hospital?"

"Since today," I squeaked out.

"Interesting timing."

I bit my lip, but since he hadn't phrased it in the form of a question, I didn't feel compelled to answer.

Raley looked from me to the doorway to Nicky's room. "You just came from that room?"

I nodded. Slowly.

"Nicky Williams's room?"

"Is it?" I asked, all mock innocence.

Raley's eyes narrowed into fine slits. "Listen, Hartley. Nicky has a severe concussion. He was attacked by someone who meant to put him out of commission."

I swallowed hard. "I know. I saw."

"Then you know this is not some game. Until we find out what happened to Nicky, I don't want to see you anywhere near him."

"But I'm this close to finding out who killed Sydney," I said, stretching the truth just a little.

Raley cocked his head to one side. He took a step forward. Then in his most fatherly voice said, "Hartley, I'm sorry, kid, but Sydney killed herself."

I shook my head, feeling my hair whip my cheeks. "You're wrong. It was Twittercide."

His eyebrows headed north. "It was what?"

"Never mind. Look, she was killed. I'm sure of it. Nicky being hit practically proves it!"

"Nicky being hit means he was in the wrong place at the wrong time. You kids shouldn't be in the park after dark."

"Seriously? You're calling this a coincidence?"

Raley crossed his arms over his chest. "Well, as far as I can tell, the only thing Nicky and Sydney have in common is you." He shot me a pointed look.

"Me?" I squeaked out. "You can't possibly think I had anything to do with this."

"What I think is that you have a serious problem minding your own business." And with that, he grabbed my upper arm and steered me toward the elevator.

"Where are we going?"

"Home."

"But—" I started.

But Raley shut me up with one look, his evil eye staring down at me.

I clamped my lips together. Fine. The joke was on him. I needed a ride home anyway.

I sat in silence in the front seat of Raley's beige sedan, trying hard not to inhale the stale scent of a hundred stakeouts lingering in the cheap fabric seats. The smell was somewhere between the locker room at the gym and the cafeteria when they forgot to take the garbage cans out after Meat(ish)loaf Monday. Luckily, it was a short drive, and I took in deep breaths of fresh air as soon as Raley opened the passenger-side door and propelled me up the walk to my front door.

Mom had it open before I even hit it, a sure sign that Raley had called ahead.

"Oh, Hartley, what have you done this time?" she asked, coming in for a hug.

"Geez, Mom, you make it sound like the police are always bringing me home." Which was hardly fair considering it had been at least a good fifteen hours since it had last happened.

"She's fine," Raley assured her. "But I'd suggest keeping a close eye on her over the next few days. At least until we find out who attacked that boy in the park last night."

Oh, that was a low blow. Calling in the SMother? As if I needed more parental supervision.

"Oh, don't worry. I will!" Mom said. With just a little too much gusto if you'd asked me. I had a bad feeling Quinn's grounding was going to look like a picnic next to my life.

"And thank you for bringing her home," Mom continued.

"No problem." Raley shot me a look. "I'm confident it will be the last time."

I'm glad someone was.

"Can I thank you with a plate of cookies?" Mom asked. "They just came out of the oven."

I was about to warn Raley that if they were Mom's cookies, they were likely gluten-free, fat-free, dairy-free, and loaded with flaxseed, but considering the way he'd just sealed my fate with Warden Mom, I decided to let him fend for himself.

"Thanks, actually a cookie sounds great," he said, following Mom into the kitchen.

On the downside, Raley was in my house. On the upside, it was the first time in days I'd seen Mom apart from her computer.

Not surprisingly, Mom put me on lockdown until the "park attacker" was caught. Which sucked because, with Raley barking up the wrong tree, I was pretty much the only one looking for the real attacker. Which I couldn't do from my bedroom. I hate irony.

With lockdown mode firmly in place, Mom insisted on not only driving me to school but actually walking me to my first class. I kept my head down and prayed no one would notice.

It wasn't until lunch that I had a chance to tell Sam and Kyle what had happened at the hospital. I caught up to the two of them in the cafeteria. Only, as I approached their table with my tray, I realized they weren't alone. Chase was sitting next to Kyle, laughing about something on Kyle's phone.

I bit my lip. I hadn't seen Chase since the awkward non-date at Pizza My Heart. While I thought I'd played off the I'm-totally-not-overdressed-and-date-ready-for-you thing then, I still felt a blush hit my cheeks as I remembered my foray into Idiotville thinking he had possibly been interested in me. I took a deep breath, trying to diffuse the heat in my face, and walked toward the table as confidently as I could.

Chase spotted me first, but if he had any inkling of the awkward controlling my every movement, he didn't betray it. "Hey," he said, scooting his tray over to make room for me.

I set mine down, doing my best to eradicate the awkward from my voice as I returned his "Hey."

"Hart, check out the shirts I had made!" Sam said, gesturing to her chest.

I looked down. Today Sam and Kyle were wearing matching red ones with big gold half hearts on each.

"Cute."

"Oh, wait for the full effect. . . ." She nudged Kyle in the ribs and he moved in close, putting his arm around her shoulders. Sam put her arm around his back, and with the two of them close together, the two heart halves on their shirts came together to make a whole.

"Okay, that is actually kinda clever," I admitted.

Sam beamed. "Ashley Stannic took our picture after

second period and said she was putting us in her column as the Herbert Hoover High Honeys of the week. How cool is that?"

Chase smirked and shook his head at Kyle. "I can't believe you let her dress you, dude."

Sam stuck her tongue out at him before turning to me and doing an artful subject change. "So, what did Nicky say yesterday?"

I quickly filled them in while I dug into my platter of chicken nuggets (our lunch lady's version of "Wings Wednesday").

"So, Nicky's too scared to talk?" Chase asked when I'd finished.

I nodded. "Yep."

"But clearly someone is after him."

I nodded again. "Clearly."

"And chances are it's the same someone who went after Sydney," Sam added.

"Be quite a coincidence if it wasn't," Chase said, mirroring my own words to Raley yesterday.

"I guess that means that Sydney's Twittercide does have to do with the cheats after all," Sam said.

"Which puts both Quinn and Connor in the clear," Kyle observed.

I thought about this, chewing on a nugget. "Not necessarily."

"What do you mean?" Chase asked, grabbing a nugget from my plate.

I moved my tray out of his reach. "I mean, what if Quinn was the person stealing the cheats in the first place?"

Sam raised an eyebrow at me. "Could that be?"

"Why not? Sydney gave up that Quinn was in on the cheating scandal, but what if what she didn't say was that Quinn was the one behind the whole thing? Maybe Sydney found out that Quinn was the one supplying the answers to Nicky in the first place. Maybe that's what Nicky was going to tell me that night, only Quinn whacked him from behind before he could."

"Brilliant!" Sam said. "Let's go bust Quinn."

"Hold on there, Sherlock," Chase said, putting a hand on Sam's arm. "How would Quinn get the answers?"

I chewed the inside of my cheek. "I dunn—" I stopped myself just in time from saying the forbidden word in his presence. "We'd have to find that out," I hedged instead.

I thought I saw the corner of Chase's lip quirk up ever so slightly, but it might have been my imagination.

"Well then, what about Connor?" Kyle suggested.

"What about him?" I asked.

"Couldn't he be the guy with the answers?"

I shrugged. "I guess. But then why would Sydney go through all the trouble of buying them from Nicky if her boyfriend had them all along?"

"Maybe she didn't know," Sam said, jumping on the theory. "Maybe it wasn't until she bought them from Nicky that she figured out where they came from. And once Connor dumped her, maybe she wanted a little revenge. Maybe she was going to blow the whistle on him, and he killed her before she could."

"Or," I said, getting into the swing of things, "what if it was Jenni? What if she got the answers, then sold them to Sydney to set her up so she could get Connor!" I'll admit it, I really wanted the twit with the big hair to be the bad guy.

"There's just one small problem with all these harebrained theories," Chase said.

"And what would that be?" Kyle asked.

"How did they get the answers to the test in the first place?"

I bit my lip. Good point. "Mr. Tipkins said he keeps his answers in a locked cabinet in his classroom," I pointed out. "I'd guess most of the other teachers do the same. And if their cabinets look anything like Tipkins's ancient thing, they're not exactly vaults, you know? Anyone could have broken in and stolen them."

"But wouldn't the teachers notice? I mean, if the locks were broken on their file cabinets?" Sam said.

"Maybe whoever was stealing the answers didn't break the locks. Maybe they just picked them."

Chase paused, then nodded. "I suppose it's possible. But wouldn't someone have seen them?"

"Not if they went in at night," Kyle offered. "No one's around then. They could have broken into the school, slipped into the classroom, picked the lock, and copied the test answers with no problem."

"This is a lot of 'could have' and 'maybe,'" Chase pointed out. "It's easy to say someone broke into the school, but how easy would it really be to do?"

I had a bad feeling I was going to regret this but . . . "I think we need to find out."

Three pairs of eyes turned my way.

"What do you mean?" Sam asked slowly, even though I could tell by the way her eyes were narrowing at me that she had a pretty good idea what I meant.

"Well," I said, clearing my throat with a bravado that I most certainly did not feel, "I think we need to find out how easy it is to break into the school at night. By breaking in ourselves."

"Dude!" Kyle said.

Chase just grinned. "You are a baaaaaad girl, Hartley Grace Featherstone," he said.

Coming from him that sounded like a compliment.

Even worse . . . I kinda liked it.

We all agreed to meet up in front of the school beneath the shaded oak tree after dark.

Which, I realized, was easier said than done.

As soon as school got out, Mom was parked at the curb, windows open, her stereo blasting Aerosmith. I made for the car at a dead run, then slumped down in my seat, shooing her away from the curb before every single person in San Jose heard her screeching power ballad.

Once home, Mom made me do my homework in the kitchen, where she could "keep an eye on my safety." One macroburger and edamame fries dinner later, I was still trying to figure out how to slip away from the SMother.

I had snuck out of my room after dark once or twice before but only in emergencies. There was the one time that I'd hopped out of my bedroom window and the other time I'd gone up into the attic, out that window, and then slid down the roof until I hit the top of Mom's minivan. But Mom had found out about both routes, first installing an alarm on my window, then boarding up the one in the attic. Which left precious few ways out of the house.

There was one window in Mom's room, but I realized as I snuck down the hallway to check it out while Mom was in the bathroom, the two-story drop was a no-go. A large oak tree grew just a few feet away, but I'd have to be either a spider monkey or Spider-Man to reach it from her room.

Which left just one alternative: the front door.

I waited an agonizing eternity while she cleaned up dinner and tidied the kitchen, then sent me upstairs to my room and settled herself in the living room to watch the cooking channel with her laptop. I paced my carpeted floor, listening to the muted sounds of the TV, and watching the sun sink lower and lower in the sky, until our backyard was bathed in deep, inky blues.

It was dark. Everyone would be waiting for me. I had to get out.

I peeked around the corner of the stairwell.

Mom was tucked under an afghan on the sofa, her laptop perched on her knees, fingers flying. Then they paused. Mom giggled. Then she began typing again. Paused. Giggled.

I rolled my eyes. Mom was IM'ing with Mr. Cyber Wonderful again.

On the one hand, this was so wrong. I mean, Mom was way too old to be giggling. It wasn't good for her. Who was this guy she was chatting with, anyway? He could be anyone—some pervert, a stalker, a serial killer. While we had regular lectures at our school about cyber safety, I was afraid Mom's generation knew next to nothing.

On the other hand, the distraction was just what I needed.

At the base of the stairs sat the kitchen on one side and the living room on the other. At the far end of the living room was the front door. I'd have to somehow cross the entire room and open the door without Mom seeing me.

I did a deep breath and took one tentative step down the carpeted stairs, then paused, listening for any sounds of protest from Mom. Nothing. I took another and another. I was now completely exposed. If Mom turned around, I was going to have to do some fancy explaining about why I was dressed in all black just to sneak downstairs for a bedtime snack. I quickly stepped down the last of the stairs, and ducked to my knees, falling to the floor behind the back of the sofa.

Mom was just on the other side. I could hear her breathing over the sounds of her keyboard clacking. I made my own breath as shallow as I could, slowly moving one leg then the other, making a snail's pace as I crawled across the room. I could see the front door. I was just a few feet away. If I could cross to it without making a sound, I had a fighting chance of getting out.

Slowly, painstakingly, I crawled the length of the sofa. At one point, Mom stretched, and I swear I almost had a heart attack. But she didn't turn around, instead laughing out loud at something her cyber guy said.

So age inappropriate.

I slowly continued my trek until I hit the end of the sofa. Then, I crawled low to the ground toward the door, ducking behind a pillar as I reached up for the front knob.

I turned, one half inch at a time, slowly, waiting for just the right moment, when the TV switched to a noisy commercial for OxiClean, to turn the knob all the way to the right until the telltale click sounded. I pulled the door open an inch, then another, cringing as it squeaked.

But by some miracle of miracles, Mom was so engrossed in her conversation that she didn't turn around. I took the opportunity and quickly slipped outside, shutting the door with a soft click behind me.

Then I dashed across the front lawn at sprinter speeds, half expecting Mom to come rushing after me. I didn't stop running until I hit the end of the block.

Phase One: down. Operation Escape Mom was a success.

I slowed to a walk, letting my breathing return to normal as I quickly headed toward school.

Now, on to Phase Two.

I only hoped that breaking into the high school went as smoothly as breaking out of Mom's.

FIFTEEN

OUR SCHOOL WAS BUILT IN THE 1920S, DECORATED WITH huge stone columns and a neoclassical design that made it look like a cross between the White House and a Roman palace during the day. At night, however, it was lit from below, cast with an eerie glow that made it look like a giant white mausoleum squatting in the middle of downtown.

A pair of ancient oak trees flanked the stone building, and as I made my way across the front lawn, I saw Sam, Kyle, and Chase standing under one, Sam dancing nervously from foot to foot.

"What took you so long?" she asked as I approached their group. I noticed they'd each gone with the same wardrobe theme I had: all black. Sam and Kyle were in matching hoodies. Chase? Honestly, he didn't look a whole lot different than any other day, in black jeans and a black long-sleeved T.

"Sorry," I told them. "Had to sneak past Mom."

"Tell me about it," Sam said, rolling her eyes. "I had to promise Kevin two tubes of cookie dough to distract my parents while I slipped out the back door."

"Are we ready to do this?" Chase cut in, all business.

Sam bit her lip, did some more dancing around on the damp grass. "Sorta. Kinda."

"Sam, you okay?" I asked.

"Well, it's just that . . . if I get caught, this is going on my permanent record. Plus, I'm pretty sure my dad will kill me."

"We're not going to get caught," Chase reassured her.

"How can you be so sure?"

"I'll tell you what," I said. "How about you stay here as lookout, okay? That way, if anything goes down, you can bolt. No permanent-record blemish." Not that I was counting on anything going down. I was pretty sure Mom would kill me, too, if she found out what I was up to.

Sam looked from Chase to me. "Okay, I'll be lookout. But I'm not bolting. I wouldn't do that to you."

I gave her a quick hug. "Thanks."

"Maybe I should stay here, too," Kyle said, eyeing the school building.

I shot Kyle a look.

"Dude, I don't think it's safe to leave Sam here alone in

the dark. Not after what happened to Nicky."

While I had a feeling that Nicky had been specifically targeted and since Sam had no idea who was selling the cheats, she was pretty safe, what he said made a certain sense. And, honestly, it was kinda cute that he was worried about her.

"I guess that leaves you and me, Hart," Chase said. "Ready to break and enter?"

I gulped down a small amount of fear, said good-bye to my own stain-free permanent record, and nodded. "Ready."

Step one was simple: get inside the school. Chase and I tried the obvious route first, but as we'd expected, the front doors to the school were firmly locked in place. Lucky for us, there were about a billion other entrances. We circled the main building, coming to the back quad, where the ancient Roman part of our school met up with the modern math and science wings. Unfortunately, the first couple of doors I tried in the math wing were locked, too.

"So, your plan is to try every door on campus on the off chance someone forgot to lock one?" Chase asked.

I paused, hand on doorknob number five (locked). He had a point. Our whole purpose here was to prove that it was so easy to break into the school and steal the answers that anyone could do it. Most likely our cheat stealer hadn't checked every door, hoping that one was open. Most likely he or she had a more foolproof way in.

Like picking a lock.

Luckily, contrary to what Chase might think, I was prepared for that.

I slipped my hand into my sweatshirt pocket, coming out with a hairpin I'd plucked from Mom's room. I stuck the end in my mouth, biting off the rubber tip, then did my best to straighten it out into one long piece of metal.

"What's that?"

"Hairpin."

Chase raised an eyebrow as I stuck it into the keyhole at the front of the handle. "You done this before?" he asked.

"Nope."

"You know what you're doing?"

"I watched a YouTube video this afternoon."

I thought I heard Chase snort behind me, but I was too intent on the keyhole to turn around. Instead, I wiggled the piece of metal up and down, side to side, slowly moving it in any direction I could just like the guy on the video. Too bad I had no idea what I was feeling for. And, unlike the guy on the video, five minutes later the door was still locked.

"Got a plan B?" Chase asked.

I blew a big breath of air up toward my hair, straightening and looking around the campus.

Truth was I did not. I spent most of my life trying to

get out of school. Breaking in had never been high on my list of priorities.

I looked up at the main building. This part of the school was two stories high, though the east and west wings, which had been added on later, were only one story. Behind us sat rows of portables. In all, there were over a hundred classrooms, most dark at this hour.

Most.

As I squinted across the quad, I noticed a light in one of the windows of the science wing.

"There," I said pointing. "Someone's inside."

Chase spun around. "I hate to break it to you, but it's probably just the custodian."

I bit my lip, watching as a figure moved in the room. Right. The custodian. Who was in there mopping experiments gone wrong off the floors, wiping notes off the whiteboards, and taking out the trash. And who probably had a set of keys to get in . . .

"That's it! I know how the cheat thief got in!"

Chase raised another eyebrow at me. "Don't tell me you think the custodian is stealing the answers?"

I shook my head. "No. But he has to get in and out of the building, right? To take out the trash and stuff?"

Chase nodded. "I guess."

"So when he goes in and out, you think he pauses to lock the door behind him each time?"

A tiny grin played at the corners of Chase's mouth. "I doubt it. He probably just locks everything up when he's done."

"Which means some of the doors must be unlocked while he's working."

"Let's go check it out."

We quickly crossed the quad, staying out of the line of any outdoor lighting, then moved close to the building as we approached the science wing. I ducked under the window with the light on, peeking just my eyes and nose above.

As we'd guessed, a custodian was in the room. Big guy with buzz-cut hair and a pair of coveralls on. He had earbuds in, his mouth moving to the music as he dipped a gray mop into a bucket and swished it along the floor.

Chase tapped me on the shoulder, then pointed to the left. Two windows down there was a door. I nodded, following him as he crouch-walked toward it.

He stuck a finger to his lips in a silencing motion as he slowly tried turning the knob.

What do you know? It opened easily in his hand.

I did a silent *yes* and a fist pump as we slipped inside.

The hallways were eerily quiet, the only sound a rhythmic ticking of a clock encased in a protective metal cage on the wall. I blinked, letting my eyes adjust to the dark as I got my bearings. The good news was that we were inside the school. The bad news was that Mr. Tipkins's room was in the math wing, on the opposite side of the building.

Chase led the way as we slowly walked the length of the corridor and turned right at the end of the hall to enter the main building.

It was even darker here, the ancient architecture not affording much natural light as all the windows were high and tiny. I squinted through the darkness, doing my best to make out familiar shapes. A water fountain outside Spanish. A bank of lockers at the end of the hall. A poster about the upcoming homecoming dance on the wall next to the trophy case.

I put my hands out in front of me, feeling my way through the building as I followed Chase.

Ten dark, stumbling minutes later (I know because I pulled my cell out to light the way as we rounded the corner to the math wing), we finally hit the door to Mr. Tipkins's classroom.

Where we encountered another lock.

"Still got that hairpin?" Chase asked.

I nodded, pulling it from my pocket and sticking it into the keyhole.

But fifteen minutes later, I was still wiggling the hairpin to no avail. And I was beginning to seriously rethink our theory about how the cheats had gotten out. Okay, it was possible that the thief was a lot better at picking locks than I was. It was possible he had better tools than a bent hairclip from his mom. But it was growing less likely by the second.

I almost jumped out of my skin when my phone buzzed in my pocket. I pulled it out to see a text from Sam.

whats taking so long?

locked door, I responded.

hurry. cold out here.

I slipped my phone back in my pocket and found Chase leaning over to scrutinize the lock.

"You know, maybe we don't have to pick it," he said.

I raised an eyebrow his way. "What do you mean?"

"Well, the locks aren't state of the art. In theory, all we have to do is slip something between the latch in the handle and doorframe plate, and it should slide open."

I blinked at him.

"I watched a couple YouTube videos, too," he confessed. "Got a credit card?"

I shook my head. "My allowance is twenty bucks a month. I'm not exactly on Visa's list of high rollers."

Chase shrugged, then reached into his back pocket and pulled out his wallet. He slipped his driver's license from its slot and turned to the lock.

"Here goes nothing," he said under his breath as he slipped just the edge of the card into the doorjamb. It went in easily enough, so he slipped the rest of its length in, holding on to a small edge. Then he slowly slid the card lower, angling it in toward the door. He turned the handle and pushed.

Only nothing happened.

"Admit it," I said, blowing out a breath of frustration. "We have lock pick fail."

"Patience, grasshopper." He tried again, sliding the card up and down, trying to finesse the latch from its housing.

Grasshopper was just about to give up and go back to her cold friends outside when I heard a click and Chase's license slid lower than before. He froze, then slowly pushed on the door.

And it opened.

He turned to me, and in the dark I could see his teeth gleaming brilliant white as a grin spread across his face.

I should never have doubted him.

"Ladies first," he said, holding the door open for me.

"*Gracias.*" I stepped into the room and pulled out my cell phone to provide some illumination. Maybe it was the dim lighting making my other senses stronger, but the room smelled different in the empty darkness. Like pungent dry-erase markers and mildewing books. I took in shallow breaths, quickly going to the file cabinet Mr. Tipkins had told me held all his test copies.

I pulled at the cabinet door. Locked.

I was getting really tired of all the locks.

Chase pulled out our trusty hairpin again and went to work, jiggling it into the hole.

I wandered over to Mr. Tipkins's desk, feeling like I was in forbidden territory. The top was littered with papers, some marked with grades at the top in red pen, others still waiting to be given sentencing. I couldn't help peeking a little. I shifted the papers, looking at the graded ones. It looked like Chris Fret was failing this class, too (poor guy!), but amazingly, Connor had gotten an A on the last test. Which immediately put him higher on my list of suspects. He hadn't struck me as the brainiac type.

I moved on to Mr. Tipkins's desk drawers, trying the top one first. It opened easily (no way, something in this school was actually unlocked?), revealing a stash of pens (mostly red), paper clips, some gum, and a couple pieces of hard candy that looked like they might have been there since the school was built. I moved on to the next drawer down, finding a stapler, hole punch, and a couple more boxes of pens. The third drawer held a paper bag that, if the stench was any indication, contained a long-forgotten lunch. I quickly shut it, trying not to breathe too deeply, and pulled open the bottom drawer. Inside were more student papers, crinkled and unorganized. I shuffled a couple (wondering who else in the class might be getting grades that were *too* good) and saw a flash of metal at the bottom of the drawer.

A key.

"Chase?"

"Just a minute. I've almost got it open."

"Think this would help?"

"What?" Chase spun around.

I held the key out to him on one finger, unable to help the grin I could feel spreading across my face.

"Where did you find that?"

"Desk drawer."

He grunted like he wished he'd thought of looking there himself, then grabbed the key. Which, I was happy to see, slipped easily into the lock.

Chase turned it, and the file drawer slid open, revealing every test that Mr. Tipkins had ever given.

"Bingo," I said. "Anyone could have broken in here."

Chase nodded, handing the key back to me. "Anyone with YouTube and a credit card."

"Or a driver's license," I pointed out, putting the key back in Tipkins's drawer.

My phone buzzed in my pocket again.

"Geez, hold your horses, Sam," I muttered as I pulled it out.

Only this text wasn't complaining about the cold weather.

someone coming!

Uh-oh.

"Uh, Chase? Sam says someone is—"

But I didn't get to finish as Chase grabbed me by the arm, pulling me to the floor. "Someone's coming," he whispered.

Sure enough, the light in the hallway outside flipped on, and I heard the click of footsteps echoing through the corridor.

And stopping just outside Mr. Tipkins's classroom.

SIXTEEN

MY EYES WHIPPED AROUND THE ROOM FOR SOMEWHERE TO hide. Under a desk? At the back of a cabinet? Behind the poster of the seven different types of triangles?

Chase must have done the same thing as he grabbed me by the arm. "Quick. In here," he said, pointing to a supply closet at the back of the room. Thank God it was left unlocked at night, and the door opened easily as Chase shoved me in front of him then stepped inside, quickly closing it behind him.

Just as we heard the door to Mr. Tipkins's room open.

I sucked in a breath in the stuffy dark space. It was small, just big enough for the two of us to fit, though not big enough to afford either of us any personal space. Meaning Chase's body was right up against mine, creating a warm, unsettling feeling in my belly that felt very . . . personal.

As I tried to decide if I liked the feeling or not, the classroom light turned on.

I shifted to look through the crack in the closet door, feeling Chase do the same beside me. (Very close beside me, causing his leg to rub against my leg in a way that had me leaning slightly closer to a "liking it" decision.)

A figure moved across my field of vision, and for a quick moment, I thought maybe we had been lucky enough to catch the cheat stealer in the act. But as he shifted to the right, I saw a familiar plaid, short-sleeved, button-down shirt and pair of baby-poo brown corduroy slacks cross the room.

Mr. Tipkins.

I closed my eyes and said a silent prayer that he didn't need any supplies tonight as he moved to his desk and sat down. He grabbed the stack of uncorrected papers I'd seen earlier and shoved them into a brown leather briefcase with scuff marks along the edges. He opened his top drawer and grabbed a couple red pens. Then he pulled a couple papers from the desk, uncapped a pen, and started marking.

Oh no. Please tell me he's not settling in for a night of correcting papers here!

I shifted, my right leg rubbing against Chase again.

The air in the closet was getting warm. It was dusty and smelled like old wood.

Though I noticed, as the minutes stretched on, there

was another scent mingling with the old closet smells, too. Fabric softener, soap, and a faint woodsy smell that was surprisingly like the men's department at Macy's. Cologne? Body spray? Deodorant? Whatever it was, I found myself not entirely hating being stuck in the closet with Chase.

He shifted, his body pressing up against mine, and I felt the lean muscles of his chest against my arm, his breath warm on my neck. Irrationally, I started thinking of all the things we could do in a dark closet together to pass the time while Tipkins corrected.

I wasn't sure how much time passed, but my left foot was starting to fall asleep (crowded up against a stack of textbooks), and the air in the closet was getting seriously warm (or maybe that was just me. Was it my imagination or was Chase leaning closer?), when I felt Chase's breath tickle my skin.

"Tipkins is moving."

I looked through the crack in the door, forcing myself to focus despite the way too personal quarters. Chase was right. Mr. Tipkins had gotten up from the desk and was moving . . . toward the filing cabinet.

"You locked the cabinet, right?" I whispered.

I felt Chase shake his head. "I didn't have time."

Oh, fudgecakes.

I watched, dread curling around in my belly as Mr. Tipkins leaned down to unlock the cabinet. He stuck the key in the hole, turned, then frowned. His bushy eyebrows furrowed together as the realization hit that the cabinet was already unlocked.

He straightened up, glancing over both shoulders, surveying the room for a possible answer as to why it was open.

I shrank as small as I could, hoping he didn't see the guilt emanating from the closet.

Luckily, he simply shoved the key into his pocket and opened the cabinet. He removed a couple sheets of test answers, stuck them in the briefcase, then shut and locked the cabinet. He dropped the key back in his desk, then gathered the briefcase in his hands and walked out of the room.

A second later the light went off, and I let out a sigh of relief as I heard footsteps retreating down the hall.

"That was close," I whispered.

"Yeah," Chase said. I could feel his breath coming hard beside me.

"Think it's safe to leave the closet?"

"Probably." But he didn't move.

"So . . . do you want to?"

"Not really. I kinda like it in here."

I rolled my eyes in the dark and shoved him out ahead of me.

Even though part of me kinda agreed.

* * *

Fifteen minutes later, we were outside again, jogging around the far side of the school to where Sam and Kyle were still standing under the oak tree. Though it was hard to distinguish one figure from the other as they were firmly stuck together at the lips.

"Ahem!" I said in an exaggerated throat clearing.

Sam detangled her tongue from Kyle's long enough to look up. "Oh. Hey."

"Hey," I said. "You guys are supposed to be our lookouts not make-outs."

Sam blushed in the moonlight. "You guys were taking forever. We had to find a way to keep warm out here."

I rolled my eyes.

"Besides," she pointed out, "we did warn you someone was coming."

"Did he see you?" Kyle asked.

I shook my head, relaying our brush with Tipkins.

"But you found the test answers?" Kyle pressed when I was done.

Chase nodded. "Yeah. The custodian is the way in. As long as you go in a door he's opened, it's unlocked. I'm guessing it's the same every night."

"And the file cabinet was easy to get into. The key is in Mr. Tipkins's desk."

"So, really, the only lock you'd have to pick is the one

to the classroom," Chase added.

"And Chase got in there, no problem," I said, telling them how he'd used his driver's license.

"So, anyone could have stolen the answers?" Sam said when I was done.

I nodded. "Right. Meaning any one of our suspects could be the person who killed Sydney over them."

Which left just one very important question: Which one was it?

SEVENTEEN

THAT QUESTION PLAGUED ME THE ENTIRE WALK BACK HOME as I considered the info we'd gathered over the last week. Clearly the test answers were the key to who had killed Sydney. But how had she found out who was stealing them? Did she know the thief personally? Was it one of her friends? Or an enemy? Clearly I was missing something here, and the empty spot where that something should be was burning a hole in my brain.

The next day, Mom agreed to drop me at the front entrance of school and not walk all the way in. (Thank God!) I felt slightly guilty that her trust in me was based on the erroneous assumption that I'd been tucked up in my room all last night like a good prisoner. But only slightly. (She had, after all, tortured me with Bon Jovi at top volume the whole ride to school.)

As soon as I walked into the main building, I saw a table set up in the hall with a clipboard of names and a cardboard ballot box on top. Jessica Hanson was manning it, handing out little slips of paper to anyone who passed by.

"Hartley!" she hailed me. "Have you voted yet?"

"Voted?"

"For homecoming court. Duh!" Jessica rolled her eyes at me.

I had to admit I hadn't.

"Today's the last day," Jessica said, handing me a slip of paper as she crossed my name off her clipboard.

"Wait—today?" I asked. "I thought we had until Thursday?"

Jessica did another eye roll, and I could see she'd doubled up on the blue eyeliner today. "Earth to Hartley? Today is Thursday."

I blinked at her. Really? I'd been so caught up in trying to track down Sydney's killer that I'd totally blanked out the rest of the world. If today was Thursday, that meant that the big football game was tomorrow and the homecoming dance the next night.

Not, mind you, that I was planning on going. Dances, especially homecoming dances, were a date kind of thing, and considering I was currently guy-less, I'd planned on a nice quiet night at home with a package of Oreos instead. I looked down at the slips of paper next to Jessica's ballot box. Four guys and three girls were named. I noted with a pang the conspicuously empty spot where Sydney's name might have been. Beside the remaining nominees were empty circles to fill in for king and queen. At the very bottom there was a spot for a write-in vote.

I looked at my choices. There was a football player/cheerleader couple that looked like they probably stood a good chance. There was a Color Guard girl and soccer player combo that could be a close second. Then there was the Connor, Jenni, and Ben trio. My money was on Connor and Jenni. But honestly? I really didn't want them to win. Something about the way they'd played girlfriend musical chairs just to get the vote hit me the wrong way. So I decided to have a little fun and write in a couple instead. I dropped the ballot in Jessica's box and headed toward first period.

I was halfway there when my cell buzzed in my pocket. I pulled it out just outside lit class.

it's jenni. we need 2 talk.

I quickly texted her back.

about?

connor.

I raised an eyebrow. I wasn't sure what Jenni could tell me about Connor that I didn't already know, but I was certainly interested in listening.

@ lunch? I asked.

sure. meet @ *bucks.

cool. c u then

I flipped my phone shut just as the bell rang and quickly joined the swarm of people dispersing to their classrooms.

The Starbucks on Blossom Hill Road is only three miles from school, which is nothing if you are lucky enough to have a car. And a heck of a hike if you're not. Thankfully, Sam had borrowed the Green Machine that day and was more than happy to give me a ride if a pre-lacrosse-practice caffeine fix was in the mix.

It was one of the larger coffee places in town, decorated in a trendy-chic style that was supposed to make people feel good about spending four dollars on a cup of coffee. Personally, if said coffee was full of creamy syrupy goodness, I thought it was well worth it. Tables lined the walls, filled with people on laptops.

In the center of the room was a circular booth surrounded by tables on all sides where soccer moms chatted in their workout clothes and older couples sat reading books. A few smaller tables dotted the rest of the floor space, and I noticed a blond woman sitting by the windows who kept looking up every time the door opened.

I blinked as she turned her profile our way.

Wait a minute. . . .

"Mom?" I asked.

Mom blinked across the room at me, surprise hitting her face for a second before a smile replaced it and she waved me over. "Hartley!"

I crossed the crowded room, Sam a step behind me.

"Mom, what are you doing here?" I asked, suddenly insanely worried she'd somehow caught wind of my lunch meeting.

A worry that I realized was completely unfounded as she answered, "I'm meeting someone for coffee."

I narrowed my eyes. "Someone?"

She looked down at her napkin. "Uh-huh."

"A male someone?"

"Sort of."

"From the internet?"

"Well . . ."

"Mom!"

"What?" she asked, putting out her hands palms up. "Match dot com says that coffee is a perfect first date."

"You're here on a date?" This was much more worrisome than being followed.

She pulled herself up to her full height, despite the hot pink color spreading from her cheeks to her forehead. "Yes. I'm waiting for my date."

"This is a disaster. You can't date!"

"Hartley, don't you think you're overreacting just a little?"

"What do you know about this guy?" I asked, ignoring

her. "What if he's crazy? What if he's some psycho?"

"Hartley," she said, giving me a head tilt. "He's not a psycho. I know him well enough to be sure of that."

"You can't really get to know anything about a guy through IM, Mom."

"Which is why we're meeting in person for coffee," she said.

I pursed my lips together. "Are you sure you don't want to take up knitting?"

"Hartley!"

"Fine!" I threw my hands up. "I'm just gonna go sit in the corner now and pretend I don't know you. But," I added, "if Cybercreep does anything funny, call me."

Mom grinned at me. "He's not a cybercreep, Hartley. He's a perfectly nice, normal guy."

"Yeah, they all start out that way. . . ," I said, letting the warning trail off as I jumped into line behind Sam, all the while keeping one eye on Mom. I watched as the front door opened, her eyes shooting to it with way too much excitement as a guy walked in. He was tall, dark-haired, and dressed in a suit. I held my breath as I watched him cross the room . . . then sit down at a table with another suit-wearing guy.

Whew. Not my future cyberdad.

I grabbed a skinny caramel macchiato and followed Sam to a table near the back (with a good view of Mom so

I could keep an eye on Cybercreep). Sam dug into her feast of a Venti Frappuccino with whipped cream, lemon scone, and a glazed donut.

In two minutes flat, she'd inhaled the whole thing.

"Wow," I commented.

"What?" She blinked at me.

"Hungry much?"

"Hey, this is my lunch. Besides, I need the extra calories for lacrosse," she said, licking a couple stray crumbs from her lower lip.

At this rate, all that extra exercise was going to end up adding pounds.

Thankfully, before I could comment, the front door opened again and a familiar brunette, Bumpit-enhanced hairdo walked in.

She spotted us, then pointed to the drink line. Five minutes later, caffeinated beverage in hand, she pulled a chair up to our table.

"Hey. Sorry, wicked long line," she observed.

I nodded. "You said you wanted to tell me something about Connor?" I prompted.

"Yeah." She put both elbows on the table and leaned forward. "Look, I know you think I had something to do with Sydney's death."

I paused. Was I that transparent?

"What makes you say that?"

"Hello? Other woman? Dude, I watch *CSI*, I know how this goes."

Maybe Jenni wasn't as dumb as I thought.

"Okay, the thought had crossed my mind," I admitted.

"But I didn't do it," she protested. "The truth is I'm dumping Connor."

Color me shocked. "Why?"

She sighed. "Do you know how hard it is to compete with a dead girl?"

Luckily, no. I shook my head.

"All I hear about is Sydney this, Sydney that," she continued. "Sydney was going to wear a pink dress to homecoming, and Sydney was going to thank the principal in her homecoming speech. I swear if I hear the name Sydney one more time, I'm gonna lose it. And the worst part is," she said, leaning in, "I can't even say anything about it! I mean, I can't very well put down a dead girl, right?"

I had to agree, it was a tough spot.

"That sucks," Sam sympathized.

Jenni shrugged. "I guess Connor's going through some sort of weird survivor's guilt, but it's driving me nuts and I can't take it anymore. Anyway, I just wanted you to know that I'm leaving Connor, so you can cross me off your whole suspects list. Truth is he's so not worth killing over."

That I could totally agree with.

"You don't happen to know where Connor was three nights ago, do you?" I asked.

Jenni screwed up her Proactivly-flawless face. "At home, I guess. Doing homework. We had a quiz in Tipkins's class yesterday."

I nodded. I knew. I also knew Connor had suspiciously aced it.

"About that," I said. "How is Connor doing in that class?"

Jenni sipped loudly at her coffee drink through a lipstick-stained straw. "Awesome. His study partner is Val Michaels. You know her?"

Not personally, but I'd seen her name on the school's honor roll almost every semester since freshman year.

"So Val was studying with him three nights ago?" I asked.

Jenni nodded. "They study together before every quiz or test or anything. Val is really smart and totally has a crush on Connor. She gives him all the study notes, he memorizes them, then passes with a good enough GPA to stay on the football team."

Geez, was there anyone at our school not smitten with Connor?

I was beginning to see a pattern. First he'd studied with Quinn, then Val. We knew how the study session with Quinn had ended. Had he made out with Val, too? And how had Sydney taken the news that her boyfriend was not only making out with her best friend and going to homecoming with someone else, but also "studying" with a girl who "totally" had a crush on him? Had she really been as cool with it as Connor seemed to imply?

"How about you?" Sam asked Jenni, breaking into my thoughts. "Where were you three nights ago?"

"At home," she said, slurping.

"Can anyone verify that?"

Jenni blinked, her eyes going from Sam to me. "My mom, I guess. Why?"

"Nicky Williams was attacked three nights ago."

Jenni nodded. "Yeah, I know. I got, like, fifteen 'Nicky's down' tweets."

"We think the same person who hit him also killed Sydney," Sam explained.

Jenni's eyes got big and round. "Whoa. So the killer is out there attacking other random people?"

I would hardly call Nicky random.

"Nicky was going to tell Hartley something, and we think the killer was trying to shut him up before he could," Sam clarified.

Jenni blinked at me. Then looked over both shoulders. "Wow. Maybe it's not such a hot idea that people can see me talking to you, then."

I rolled my eyes. "I think the fact that you're breaking up with Connor is not exactly news to kill over," I reassured her. I was about to tell her that I didn't think Connor was going to be that unhappy (considering he'd had the same post-homecoming plan) when a familiar figure walked in the door of the Starbucks. Tall, red-haired, packing a few extra cookies around the middle. Detective Raley.

Oh, frickin' fowl fluff.

He must have been watching me. Must have followed me here from school to meet with Jenni. Seriously? Couldn't he conduct an investigation on his own? He had to follow me to solve Sydney's Twittercide? Well, he could follow all he liked, I wasn't giving up on this story. Besides, I wasn't doing anything illegal. I was entitled to talk to my fellow students. I had journalistic rights. What amendment did those fall under again? Fourth? Fifth? Man, I really needed to study more for that American Government test.

I drew myself up as straight as I could, lifted my chin, and rehearsed a very scathing speech to give to Raley about my something-th amendment rights.

Only I didn't get to give it.

Instead of walking toward our table and giving me the leave-this-to-the-real-cops lecture I was so familiar with, Raley looked right past me, his eyes lighting up, his mouth curving into a grin that created little wrinkles at the corners of his eyes. Then he made a beeline . . .

. . . straight toward Mom's table.

Dude! Detective Raley was my mom's date?

EIGHTEEN

I FELT SICK AS I WATCHED RALEY LEAN DOWN AND GIVE Mom a peck on the cheek. This was the guy she'd been IM'ing with last night? Giggling, grinning, acting like a fool over? Ugh. Suddenly Mr. Candlelit Dinners didn't sound so bad after all.

"Whoa. Isn't that Detective Raley kissing your mom?" Sam asked.

I had to get out of there before I lost my latte. I grabbed Sam by the arm and made for the door, purposely not looking in Mom's direction again.

I spent the rest of the afternoon with that same ball of nausea in my stomach, torn between the urge to shake some sense into Mom or stick my head in the sand ostrich-style until she came to her senses. Considering Raley had a gun and I was just the teeniest bit scared of him, I went for option number two. Denial, ostrich-style.

Which worked fabulously until I spied Mom's minivan parked at the curb after school. The second I slipped into the passenger seat, Mom turned to me.

"Hartley, I think we should talk about me starting to date again."

"I really think we shouldn't."

"I know this is new. And I can see that it's upsetting to you."

"Totally not upset at all," I lied, holding on to denial with all my might. "I'm cool with it."

"Detective Raley and I got to talking the other day when he brought you home, and we realized we had a lot in common."

"You don't need to explain, Mom. I'm fine."

"I know you just see me as 'Mom,' Hartley, but I'm a woman, too."

"Mom, really. We can totally not discuss this."

"Women have certain feelings. Emotional needs. Other needs."

"Know what? Let's listen to some Steven Tyler. Really loudly, 'kay?" I begged, reaching for her radio.

Mom sighed. "Okay. But I just want you to know we can talk about this. When you're ready."

I heaved a sigh of relief as embarrassing classic rock filled the car. Discussing Mom's needs being fulfilled by

Raley was enough to make me throw myself into a pool with a charging laptop.

Thankfully, I was able to avoid Mom the rest of the afternoon, hiding out in my room as I did my homework. I even got her to agree to lift the lockdown enough to let me go to the football game the following night with Sam and Kyle by (A) pointing out that there would be plenty of teachers around and (B) telling her that I had a need to socialize with people my own age, too. (Not to mention a need to be as far away from my mom's nightly, giggling IM sessions as possible.)

So the next day after Sam and I took our dreaded American Government midterm, I went home with her to rummage in her closet for the perfect game-day outfits. Of course, Sam had to call Kyle no less than four times to make sure their outfits coordinated. I wasn't sure if it was cute or weird, but I decided to stay out of it, borrowing a hot pink sweater and a pair of black leggings that looked great with Sam's suede calf boots with the fur lining. Sam ended up in a pair of skinny jeans, her I Like Boys shirt, and a red Stanford jacket (one of several her father had purchased for her).

Kyle met up with us at the hot dog cart, where we found him wearing his Boy shirt, per Sam's orders, and shoving half a wiener in his mouth. "Hey!" He waved, wiping a glob of yellow mustard from the corner of his mouth.

"Hey," I greeted him back. Sam gave him a kiss on the cheek (the one without mustard).

"Have you seen Connor Crane?" I asked, standing on tiptoe to see over the heads of our classmates crowding into the stadium.

Kyle shook his head. "I'm sure he's here, though. He's the starting QB. Why?" he asked.

"I have a few questions for him," I answered.

With all the not thinking about Mom I'd been doing, I'd had ample time to think about our list of suspects. And I kept coming back to Connor. He'd been the closest to Sydney, and if I'd learned anything from watching cop shows on TV, it was that the boyfriend was always the prime suspect. Was Connor experiencing survivor's guilt, as Jenni had suggested? Or was it something more sinister . . . like killer's guilt?

I told Kyle and Sam my suspicions as Kyle wolfed down the rest of his hot dog. When I was done, Sam nodded.

"I agree," she said. "He's got the shakiest alibi and the biggest motive. Love makes you do crazy things sometimes."

Then, as if to illustrate her point, Sam reached up and wiped another glob of mustard from Kyle's cheek. He grinned, leaning down to kiss her.

"Ohmigod, you guys are so cute!" Ashley Stannic said, jumping in line behind us to grab a hot dog. "I'm totally writing about those shirts in my column tonight."

"Thanks!" Sam said, beaming.

"Have you seen Connor Crane?" I asked Ashley.

She nodded, her bangs bobbing up and down. "Over by the locker room. He was signing autographs for freshmen."

I thanked her and left Sam and Kyle to find us seats inside while I tracked down the quarterback.

As I slowly made my way through the crowd, I spied Chase sipping a Pepsi near the entrance to the stadium. I almost called out to him to enlist his help in interrogating Connor, but I paused. Chase was not alone. Someone was with him.

A girl someone.

An odd sensation fluttered in my belly as I took in his companion. She was tall, almost as tall as Chase, with dark hair that hung in long, loose waves like in a Pantene commercial. She was showing off her slim figure in a pair of tight, layered gray T-shirts and super skinny jeans that instantly made me aware of how bright and bulky my sweater was. I didn't recognize her from school, and she looked older . . . maybe college age? Which shouldn't have been that surprising, I guess, since Chase was a senior. It made sense he'd go for someone who was more mature.

Miss Perfect leaned in close to Chase, grabbing his arm and whispering something in his ear. Chase grinned, bursting into laughter at their inside joke.

That fluttering settled into a brick in the pit of my stomach, weighing me down so badly I couldn't raise my arm to wave at him.

Chase had a girlfriend. I felt colossally stupid for ever thinking that our mutual investigating had anything to do with going out together. Clearly Chase was already going out . . . with someone else.

I shook my head, telling myself I didn't care. Chase and I were not an item; we were nothing. We were one kiss, one time. I had no reason to feel jealous. I didn't feel jealous. I was fine. Totally fine with Chase being fine with his fine college girlfriend.

I quickly turned around and all but sprinted in the opposite direction before Chase could see me and my fineness.

So quickly that I almost knocked into Connor as he exited the locker room in front of me.

"Whoa. Dude," he said, his helmet dangling from his hand.

"Sorry."

"Ashley texted that you were looking for me?" he asked.

I was? I paused, willing my heart to slow down. Right. I was.

"Right. I was." I cleared my throat, willing my head

to focus on anything but the image of Chase's beautiful accessory. "I talked to Jenni today," I finally managed.

He gave me a frown. "Why?"

If that was a subtle jab at my social standing, I decided to ignore it. (I was getting to be an expert at this ostrich thing.)

"She told me you've been studying with Val Michaels," I said instead.

Connor cocked his head at me. "Yeah. So what?"

"How did Sydney feel about that?"

He shrugged. "I dunno. Why?"

"Well, it's just that I know how these late-night study sessions can go. I'm not sure I'd be cool with my boyfriend engaging in them. At least not after what happened with Quinn." I gave him a pointed look.

He chewed on the inside of his cheek. "Hey, that was a one-time thing. Totally a mistake. And Quinn started it."

"But Sydney wasn't very happy about it."

More cheek biting. "No."

"And then you broke up with her to win homecoming with Jenni."

"I told you, she was cool with that."

"How cool was she with you and Val studying together?"

"I dunno." He shifted his helmet to the other hand.

"I mean was she upset? Angry? Sad?"

He shrugged. "She was . . . you know . . . not happy, I guess. But she understood."

"That's a pretty understanding girlfriend," I observed. "You sure she wasn't upset? That maybe you two had an argument? One that might have gotten out of hand and someone was, say, pushed into a pool over it?"

"Dude, you are way off," Connor said. Though he shifted his helmet to the other hand again, looking distinctly uncomfortable.

"Where were you three nights ago?" I asked, switching gears.

"Why?"

"Nicky Williams was attacked. Most likely by the same person that killed Sydney."

Connor's eyes narrowed. "I had nothing to do with Nicky getting hit. I don't even know Nicky."

"And Sydney?" I pressed.

His front teeth munched down on his lower lip, his eyes hitting the ground. "Look. You want to know the truth? Fine. It was my fault, okay?"

"What was your fault?" I asked, leaning in.

"I killed Sydney."

I froze, the sudden confession stunning me. "Wait— you admit you killed her?" Surely it couldn't be this easy, could it?

Connor nodded, still staring at the ground. "She

couldn't take seeing me with Jenni. Not after what happened with Quinn. I told her it didn't mean anything, but then when she found out I was studying with Val? Well, that must have pushed her over the edge."

I narrowed my eyes. "'Pushed her over the edge?'"

He looked up, genuine regret filling his eyes. "Why else would she kill herself?"

I blinked at him. "You said you killed her because you think she killed herself over you?"

He nodded.

Mental face palm. Suddenly I wasn't sure there was enough room on the campus for both me and his ego.

On the other hand, Connor looked like he sincerely thought Sydney had killed herself over him. In fact, this was the most sincere emotion I thought I'd ever seen from him.

Which meant my number one suspect just plummeted to the bottom of my list.

I left Connor, contemplating this cheery thought as I trudged back toward the stadium. The game was about to start, but my heart just wasn't into watching it. I was depressed. Depressed for Sydney who had not only been dumped by the vainest guy in the world but also killed by some schmuck. And depressed that I was no closer to finding out who that schmuck was. It didn't seem fair.

I wandered past the main entrance gate, out into the now dark and deserted parking lot, the crowd having filtered into the stadium, where I could hear their collective cheers rising up to the night sky from the well-lit arena.

"Hart!"

I was so engrossed in being depressed that I hadn't even seen him until he called my name. Chase. He was standing at the trunk of his Camaro.

I had a fleeting thought of running away—the last thing I wanted to do was add to my depression by hearing about Chase's wonderful girlfriend—but I knew Chase could outrun me. Instead, I shoved my hands into my sweater pockets and walked toward him.

"Hey."

"How come you're not inside?" he asked.

I shrugged. "I was interviewing Connor."

"What did he say?" Chase crossed his arms over his chest, leaning against his car.

I gave him the gist of the interview, how Connor was convinced that Sydney had killed herself over him.

"Do you think she did?"

"No!" I spit out on a laugh. "Geez, how conceited can a guy get?"

Chase frowned. "Well, it's possible she was really hung up on him."

"You think all girls are just hanging on guys? That guys mean that much to us?"

Chase cocked his head at me. "No. But maybe—"

"I mean, we can get along without you guys, you know? The sun does not rise and set on having a boyfriend. Those of us without boyfriends can get along just fine."

"Okay. It was just a thought," he said, taking a step back. "Geez, what's gotten into you?"

"Nothing has gotten into me. I'm fine. Totally fine."

"O-kay."

"Where's your *friend*?" I asked.

"Who?"

"The girl I saw you with earlier."

"Oh, Carly? She's inside. She left her jacket in the car."

I looked down and saw a pink Windbreaker in his hand. Fab.

"Well, you don't want to keep her waiting," I said, turning around.

"Hart, are you okay?"

"Why wouldn't I be okay?" I shot back, a little louder than I'd meant.

"Hart—"

"I'm fine!" I shouted, then turned to go.

But I took only one step, my eyes inexplicably blinded by blurry, unshed tears, when I felt Chase's body slam into mine from behind.

"Unh!"

I fell to the ground, the full weight of Chase on top of me as the asphalt scraped my palms, and my forehead connected with the ground, jarring my teeth together with a painful smack.

I was about to ask what the hell he thought he was doing when a pair of headlights whizzed past my head, tires coming within inches of my nose.

Holy fluffin' fudge. That car had almost hit me!

NINETEEN

"DID YOU SEE THAT CAR?" CHASE GASPED IN MY EAR.

I paused, blinking back a sudden headache. "He tried to hit me. He was going to run me over."

"I didn't see the license plate, but I'm pretty sure it was a Toyota," Chase said, standing up and staring at the taillights as the car rounded the corner onto Main.

"He was going to kill me." I turned to Chase. "He was trying to kill me."

Chase reached down, grabbing my hand and pulling me up off the ground. "Did you see the driver?" he asked.

I shook my head. Honestly? I hadn't seen anything more than a pair of headlights.

"You're bleeding."

I looked down. He was right. My palms were scraped raw.

"Get in. I'll drive you home," he said, gesturing to the Camaro.

I paused. While one near-death experience was enough for one night, walking four dark blocks home while a guy in a car who wanted me dead was out there riding around didn't hold a whole lot of appeal. I did a mental eenie-meenie-minie-mo and finally got in.

Chase made the five-minute drive in two flat, pulling up to the curb outside my house and insisting on following me to the front door.

It was unlocked, and I pushed inside, finding Mom on the sofa in the living room, sitting next to the only thing that could possibly make my evening worse.

Raley.

Dude. A second date already? They both had glasses of wine in hand, and Mom's cheeks were flushed pink as if it wasn't her first.

Raley looked completely different than I'd ever seen him. Gone was Cop mode, and in its place, a relaxed pose, eyes crinkling, lips tilted upward in a lazy smile. His entire being was different.

Or maybe that was just my bump on the head talking.

"Hartley?" Mom asked, confusion lacing her voice. "I thought you were staying at Sam's."

"I fell," I said feebly.

"Someone almost ran her over," Chase corrected,

coming in behind me.

And just like that Mom went into SMother mode and Raley went into Cop mode, and I was surrounded by overprotective adults playing Twenty Questions.

"Where? What happened? Are you okay?"

They all blurred together through my headache haze. Thankfully, Chase took over, telling them about the car in the parking lot and how we'd had to dive for the pavement to avoid it. By the time he was finished, Mom was hugging me tighter than a boa constrictor, and Raley's eyebrows were doing that deep frown thing again.

"You need to be more careful," he said.

"I think this was more than just an accident," Chase said. "I think someone tried to hit her."

"Why do you think that?"

"For one? They didn't even try to brake. They just sailed through. For another, look at the sweater she's wearing. It's practically Day-Glo."

I crossed my arms over my chest and felt myself blush. Hey, not all of us can look so chic in plain gray like Miss Perfect.

"I knew I should never have let you go out alone," Mom said, crushing me to her.

"Mom. Air."

She let up a little, but shallow breaths were still all I could manage.

Raley gave me a long stare. I put on my most innocent face, just a shade shy of actually whistling and staring at the ceiling.

Luckily, he let it go.

"Look, I, uh, I have to get back to the school," Chase said.

Right. To his date.

"You gonna be okay?" he asked.

For some reason the thought of Miss Perfect waiting for him back at the stadium coupled with the concern in his voice sent that headache at my temple into overdrive. I crossed my arms over my chest.

"I'm fine," I said, hearing an edge I hadn't meant to share creep into my voice.

Chase paused, looked from Mom to Raley, then back to me. He must have decided that I was in good hands as he nodded. "Right. I'll call you tomorrow, 'kay?"

But he didn't give me a chance to answer as he turned and walked out the door.

After Chase went back to his date at the game, Mom and Raley went back to their date on our sofa (I could never sit there again), and I went to my room. Alone.

I flopped down on my bed and contemplated the ceiling, thoughts swirling in my aching head. This case was spiraling out of control faster than I could rein it in. And the ironic part was someone out there thought I knew a hell of a lot more than I did. Really? We had a lot of theories but no actual proof of anything.

Which meant, I realized as I finally drifted off to sleep, there was only one thing to do.

"I've decided to bluff."

Sam and Kyle turned to me as one over their Jamba juice. Singular. With two straws. The cute was oozing from their pores.

"Bluff what?" Chase asked, sipping through his straw and making slurping sounds.

He had, as promised, called me first thing that morning. Only I'd been too afraid of that edge creeping back into my voice to answer. I'd let him leave a message, and instead of calling him back, I'd texted Sam to tell her about my near fatal run-in with the Toyota. She had insisted on meeting me for a breakfast smoothie. And lately wherever Sam went, Kyle went. And because apparently Chase had texted Kyle to text Sam to find out why I wasn't answering my phone, Kyle had told Chase we were all meeting at Jamba Juice.

And as if the awkward, crackling in the air every time I looked Chase's way (not that he noticed, which just made me feel even more awkward), wasn't enough, guess who else had tagged along? Mom had insisted on driving me and was sitting at a table across the patio, sipping on a pre-workout wheatgrass shot while talking to my dad on the phone and sending worried looks my way every five seconds.

Which is why I had decided to do something drastic.

"I'm bluffing a story for the paper," I told the three of them.

Chase opened his mouth to protest, but I ran right over him.

"I'm going to say I'm printing a story exposing Sydney's killer."

Chase shut his mouth with a click.

"Whoa. You know who the killer is?" Kyle asked.

Sam elbowed him. "No, babe. That's the bluff part."

"Why would you do that?" Chase asked, his eyes intent on me.

I swallowed hard, trying to ignore them. "In order to get the killer to come after me."

Chase gave me a hard look. "Are you insane? Why do you want to do that?"

"How else am I going to flush this guy out?"

Chase didn't answer, just stared at me, his jaw tense, his eyes an unreadable black.

"Look," I explained, "we've been going around in circles for days. It could be Quinn, it could even still be Connor or Jenni . . . heck it could be anyone on campus! Maybe it was even Nicky and he paid someone to hit him over the head to divert attention."

"A concussion is a heck of a diversion," Kyle pointed out.

"The point is we have no idea who killed Sydney, and we're no closer to knowing than we were a week ago. So we need to do something drastic to make the killer tip his hand."

Sam nodded. "Makes sense."

"Sure, it does. The killer is already scared," Kyle said. "He killed Sydney to keep her quiet about who sold her the cheats, then hit Nicky over the head to keep him quiet, too."

"Don't forget he tried to run over Hartley," Chase said, still sending me the evil eye.

I swallowed. "Right. So if I spread the rumor that I know who the killer is and I'm going to print it in Monday's paper, it should get the killer to—"

"Come after you," Chase finished for me. He leaned forward, putting both elbows on the wire metal table. "Which is a really bad idea, Hartley."

"Not if I'm ready for him."

"How exactly do you propose to be ready?"

"Well . . ." I hadn't really thought that part through yet.

"We'll protect you," Kyle said, puffing out his chest.

"The homecoming dance is tonight," Sam piped up.

"All our suspects will be there. If we spread the rumor now, whoever is guilty will totally be on edge tonight."

"And we'll be sure to be around you twenty-four/seven. We won't take our eyes off you," Kyle repeated.

"So when the killer strikes, we'll catch him," I finished.

Sam and Kyle nodded. I nodded back. We all looked at Chase.

"Oh, now you want my opinion?" he asked, still scowling.

Not really. But I nodded anyway.

"This is the stupidest idea I've ever heard!" he said, throwing his hands in the air. "Being bait? Are you kidding me?"

"You have a better idea?"

"That's beside the point."

"Look, it will work. Trust me."

Chase narrowed his eyes. He clenched his jaw. Finally he threw his hands up. "Dammit, Hartley," he said. "Now I have to get a tux."

I blinked at him? "Tux?"

He stared right at me. "Because if you're really going to go through with this, I'm not letting you do it alone. I'm now your official homecoming date."

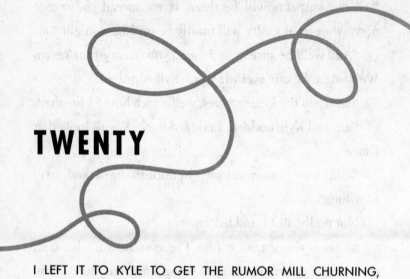

TWENTY

I LEFT IT TO KYLE TO GET THE RUMOR MILL CHURNING, watching as he sent out texts to members of the soccer team, the water polo team, and, of course, all of our prime suspects, saying:

> hart knows who killed Sydney! printin it in mon's homepage!

All we had to do now was wait for our killer to strike.

At me.

At Herbert Hoover High, homecoming was one of those things usually reserved for a certain type of girl—a girl with a date. Since I hadn't been one of those girls until this morning, there was one gaping hole in my plan to smoke out the killer there.

"I don't have anything to wear," I moaned to Sam as

soon as Kyle and Chase left to go get their rented tuxes.

"Don't worry. I'm sure I have something."

"That's even more worrisome."

She punched me in the arm. "I have excellent taste."

She was right. She did. She also had a track record of overdressing me. But, considering this was homecoming, I guess that wouldn't really be an issue, right?

Famous last words.

That afternoon, while fielding a tidal wave of incoming tweets and texts—including ones from Quinn, Connor, Drea, and Jenni—all asking if it was really true that I knew who killed Sydney, I let Sam put my homecoming outfit together. She'd grabbed from her closet the dress that she'd worn to the Valentine's formal last year, a full-length red satin with one shoulder strap and a slit up the side that reminded me of a Jessica Rabbit look. Since we were approximately the same size, it almost fit, just clinging a little tighter on me than it had her. But still, it worked.

We paired it with silver heels, a pair of faux-crystal drop earrings, and a simple silver necklace with little crystal beads in the center. While I'd insisted that Sam go light on the eye makeup, she had won the battle of the lipstick, painting my lips in the same shade of va-va-voom red as the dress. At first I'd felt like a clown, but as I looked in the mirror now, the overall effect with the dress was actually kind of nice. A little over the top, maybe, but if you couldn't go over the top for homecoming, when could you?

Sam, on the other hand, had gone a little shorter, wearing a dress with a tight-fitting purple bodice that ended in a flared, tulle skirt that came to just above her knee. It was cute and flirty and went perfectly with the purple shoes she'd dyed to match. And while I'd gone with simple understated jewelry, she'd gone big, chunky, and bling-ified. Fake diamonds hung in a teardrop shape from her ears, and an ornate necklace that looked like latticework of silver and cubic zirconia decorated her neck. Her hair was swept into an updo that was studded with a dozen tiny, clip-on faux diamonds, making her sparkle from every angle.

"Now, close your eyes," she told me, reaching into the ginormous duffel bag she'd brought over with her to dress at my house.

"Do I have to?" I protested. "I don't really like wardrobe surprises."

She put a hand on her hip. "Play along, okay? Just shut 'em."

"Fine." I felt Sam putting something on my head with little plastic teeth that dug into my scalp.

"Ow!"

"Oh, don't be such a baby," she said, arranging my hair loosely around my shoulders. "Okay, now . . . open!"

I did. And blinked at my reflection. Or, more accurately, the reflection of the mass of sparkles on my head.

"Is that a tiara?"

Sam nodded. "Uh-huh."

"It's kinda . . . sparkly, don't you think?"

She beamed, a grin taking up her whole face. "I know, right?"

"I didn't mean that in a good way."

"It's perfect."

"Sam, I'm not sure I need a tiara—"

But I didn't get to finish as Mom called up from the bottom of the stairs, "Hartley? Your date's here!"

I cringed at the term, quickly shouting back, "He's just a friend!"

Mom had done a squeal frighteningly like Sam's when I'd told her that I had changed my mind and decided to go to the homecoming dance after all. In high school, Mom had been the social butterfly, involved in everything under the sun, or so she told it, including being crowned princess of the winter ball one year. Secretly, I had a feeling she was a little disappointed that I hadn't followed in her footsteps, though she never said so. But when I had told her I was going to homecoming, her face had lit up, her voice had gone high and giggly, and she'd even lifted the lockdown despite my nearly becoming roadkill last night. Never mind that I had spent the next twenty minutes trying to tell her that, no, I did not need her to run to the florist for an emergency boutonniere (which she ignored and did anyway); no, we did not need to go get nails done and eyebrows waxed (ouch!); and no, we did not need a limo to pick us up (though this last one was tempting).

But the thing I had tried to make the most clear was that, no, Chase was not my date, just a friend who happened to be going, too. With me. At the same time. Totally different than going together.

"Hurry up, Hart. You don't want to keep your date waiting!"

"Friend!" I yelled, again.

But I was pretty sure she didn't hear me.

Sam and I grabbed our purses—hers a rhinestone-studded clutch and mine a silver, satin one—and slowly (so we didn't trip in our ridonkulously high heels) made our way down the stairs.

The first thing I saw when I rounded the corner was Chase.

And then I almost did trip.

I wasn't sure what I had expected from him for homecoming, but I'd guessed his outfit would probably involve leather, denim, or black. I was right on only one count: the black. Amazingly, Chase was dressed in a traditional tux, black on white, with a simple black tie. The effect was . . . nice. Surprising. But nice. Bordering on a hot sort of nice, even. Huh. What do you know? He cleaned up pretty good.

"Dude," Kyle said, getting an eyeful of Sam. "You look hot!"

She did a little twirl for him. "Thanks. So do you."

Sam had, as I might have guessed, coordinated matching homecoming outfits for both her and Kyle. Kyle's shirt was the exact shade of purple as Sam's dress.

"Hey," Chase said when he saw me. "You look . . . nice," he said, echoing my thoughts.

I cleared my throat, a compliment coming from Chase that was not laced in sarcasm throwing me. "Thanks." I paused. "You, too."

He gave me a slow up and down, landing on the mass of sparkles on my head. He grinned.

"One crack about the tiara and you're a dead man," I warned him.

He put up his hands in a surrender motion. "I wouldn't dream of it, princess."

I shot him a death look, but before I could spit out a scathing reply, Mom shouted, "Boutonnieres!" and emerged from the kitchen with two little plastic boxes.

I took the non-purple one and leaned in to grab Chase's lapel.

Honestly—I'd never done this before and the huge pin that came with the flower was kinda intimidating. I had a horrible vision of stabbing Chase and getting blood all over the first white shirt I'd ever seen him wear.

My hands shook a little as I slowly stabbed the front of his tux, navigating around the thick rose stem.

"Easy, Featherstone," I heard Chase whisper.

I looked up. He was grinning at me. He thought this was funny?

"Ouch!"

"Oops. My finger slipped."

He shot me a look. "I'll bet."

"Pictures!" Mom said, appearing beside me with a camera.

"Oh, Mom, we don't really need pictures," I pleaded.

"Okay, line up," she said, totally ignoring me. "Hart, move closer to Chase."

"Mom, please. I told you I don't need—"

"Chase, put your arm around your date's shoulders."

I rolled my eyes. And Mom accused me of tuning *her* out.

"That's it. Move in just a little closer so I can get you all in frame."

Chase pulled me tight against him, completely invading my personal space. His arm around my shoulders was warm, and I felt myself start to sweat in places that would stain my satin dress.

"Mom—" I pleaded again.

"Smile, Hart," Chase whispered in my ear, hamming it up as Mom popped off shots.

If I hadn't known better, I'd have sworn he was enjoying this.

After Mom had taken at least a dozen pix of us in every position possible, we all escaped out the front door . . . where Chase's Camaro sat at the curb.

"Oh, no fluffin' way." I shook my head as Sam and Kyle climbed into the tiny backseat. "You guys are kidding me, right?"

Chase looked from me to the car. "What?"

"We're going in that?" Why had I not taken Mom up on that limo thing?

"Yep." Chase beamed.

"No way."

"Why not?"

"Because I'd like to arrive at homecoming in one piece."

Chase rolled his eyes. "You have two choices here, Hart—my car or walking."

I bit my lip, tasting lipstick. I looked down at my heels. Up at his car. Back at the heels.

"Well?"

"I'm thinking!"

Chase rolled his eyes again, then walked around to the driver's side.

Without much choice, I hopped in.

On the upside, if I died on the way, at least I'd make a sparkly corpse.

The HHH cafeteria was totally transformed. Gone were the rows of Formica-topped tables, and in their place was a dance floor complete with a shimmering disco ball.

The dance's theme was Tropical Oasis, meaning potted palms were stuck in every corner, paper fish adorned the walls, and the tables lining the sides of the room were piled high with fruit and nuts, with one serving as a bar, where Pineapple Pleasure and Mango Madness were being served in small glasses complete with little umbrellas.

Several teachers were in attendance as chaperones, as well as some parents. I spotted both Sam's mom and dad taking spots near the dance floor, keeping a keen eye on Kyle. Luckily, I'd been able to "lose" the email calling for parent volunteers before my mom had read it.

The DJ fired up a Pink song, and we all jumped onto the dance floor. (Kyle made sure he kept at least an arm's length away from Sam.) I had to admit, it was kinda fun. Okay, a lot of fun. The energy was high, the music was loud, and laughter echoed off the beige walls as we all made fun of one another's dance moves.

Five songs into it, I could feel my mascara starting to sweat away, and I needed a breather.

"I'm gonna grab a drink," I said.

"What?" Chase yelled.

"I'm gonna go get a drink!"

"Huh?"

"DRINK!"

Chase nodded. "Right. Cool."

I threaded my way through the crowd, Chase a step behind me, taking his role as bodyguard seriously as we pushed through the people to the Mango Madness station. I downed my cup in almost a single gulp before getting back in line for seconds.

"Chase?"

I turned to see Chris Fret and the new guy, Michael, hailing him from across the room. "Come check this out."

Chase shook his head. "Gotta stay with my date."

"Go. I'm fine," I said, shooing him.

"No way. I'm sticking to you like glue tonight. That was the deal."

"Look around, Chase. We're surrounded by teachers. Nothing's going to happen to me at the Mango Madness table. I'll stay right here. I'm fine. Go."

Chase paused, letting the logic of that sink in. He glanced to our right. Mr. Tipkins was chatting with Ashley Stannic under a plastic palm. To our left, the Kramers were still eyeing the dance floor. Behind us, three more parents mingled with the vice principal. If the killer was going to strike, this was so the wrong moment.

"Okay," Chase finally said. "But stay here. I'll be right back. Five minutes."

I nodded. "Scout's honor."

I watched Chase jog toward Chris and Michael, then do some sort of complicated handshake thing, all three of them making fun of one another's tuxes.

I grabbed another drink, then sat in one of the chairs along the wall. I slipped a heel off, my foot immediately sighing in relief. They were hot shoes, but they were not made for dancing. Or walking. Or standing. Or anything that required my feet to be smashed into them.

I took a moment to look around as I rubbed the bottom of my foot. If I had had to guess, I'd have said at least 70 percent of the school was in attendance. I spotted Connor hanging out under a school of paper fish near the stage. Val Michaels was at his side, though I noticed his eyes were on Jenni, who was dancing with one of the football players. Apparently she'd made good on her promise to ditch Connor and had moved on already.

Just to my right were Drea and her cheerleader friends. They had a Flip cam and were shooting a video of the dance floor. I could hear her narrating the vids for Nicky.

Surprisingly, even Quinn was there, seemingly having gotten a reprieve from her grounding. She was with some guy from the water polo team, dancing near Sam and Kyle.

All our suspects were in one place. Sydney's killer had

to be in this room. The thought gave me chills despite the heat still coursing through me from the aerobic dance workout.

"Hartley," Mr. Tipkins said, coming up beside me. He'd thrown a sports jacket over his usual dumpy uniform, the elbows accented with plaid patches.

I cleared my throat. "Hi."

"How is your story coming along for the paper?"

I nodded. "Fine. Good."

"Ashley tells me she got a text saying that you know who killed Sydney."

"We're getting very close," I hedged. Which, if tonight was successful, was the truth.

He frowned. "So does that mean you also know how my test answers got out?"

I bit my lip. "Not yet, but we're almost there." Another stretch, but if the two went hand in hand like we thought they did, it was possible I might have an answer by the end of the night.

"I have a bad feeling someone may have tried to get to my tests a couple nights ago," he said.

I froze. "Uh, you do?" I asked, my voice going an octave higher than usual.

He nodded, a grave look on his face. "The door to my classroom was unlocked. As was my file cabinet."

"Really?" Minnie Mouse squeaked out.

"Really. You don't happen to have an idea who might have done that, do you?"

"Me?"

"Your voice okay?"

I cleared my throat.

"I mean, why do you think I might?" I asked, feeling a guilty blush creep up my neck.

He shrugged. "You're investigating the whole thing. I thought you might have turned up some information."

I shook my head so hard I felt my tiara go crooked. "Nope. Not me. Sorry. No idea about how that might have happened. A couple nights ago, you say? I was home. Yep, at home. Nope. Sorry."

He gave me a funny look, but nodded again. "Okay. Well, please let me know as soon as you learn anything new."

I nodded, feeling that tiara slip again.

"Yep. I totally will," I promised.

Which was almost true. If tonight went well, I'd be letting everyone know who Sydney's killer was.

TWENTY-ONE

THE REST OF THE EVENING MOVED BY IN FAST-FORWARD. WE danced some more, ate some more, then danced again, all the while keeping our eyes peeled for anyone with murderous intentions. (At one point Kyle swore Sam's dad was going to kill him for kissing her on the cheek, but that didn't really count.) Halfway through the night, the music finally stopped and Mrs. Bailey's voice came over the loudspeaker.

"Ladies and gentlemen, it's time to announce this year's Herbert Hoover High homecoming court!"

A roar went up from the crowd, everyone immediately pushing toward the front of the room.

"Before we begin," Mrs. Bailey said, hovering near a microphone center stage, "I want to take a moment to remember a former Herbert Hoover High student, Sydney Sanders."

A hush went over the crowd, instantly dropping the party level in the room about fifty notches.

"Sydney may not always have been a model student," Mrs. Bailey went on, alluding to her cheating, "but she was an enthusiastic participant in so many after-school activities, and never lacked in school spirit. So I'd like us all to take a brief moment of silence for Sydney."

She bowed her head and the audience did the same, the only sound in the echoing cafeteria the rustle of taffeta. In the silence I could almost feel the weight of finding Sydney's killer pressing down on me. He, or she, was somewhere in this room. I was sure of it.

"And now," Mrs. Bailey said moments later, breaking the silence, "on to the homecoming nominees!"

A roar of excitement went up again, almost louder than the first time, as if people needed to ramp the energy up that much higher to chase the sadness from the room.

"First we'll start with our princesses and princes," Mrs. Bailey said, reading off a piece of paper as she leaned down into the microphone. "Our first royal couple is . . . David Hech and Cori Cooper!"

I watched the soccer player–Color Guard girl combo do some fist pumping and knuckle bumping with their friends as they jogged up the steps to the stage where last year's royal court was waiting with crowns and sashes.

"Next we have . . . Jenni Pritchard and Connor

Crane! Come on up, kids!"

I scanned the room for the now non-couple. Jenni gave her date a kiss on the cheek before eagerly bounding to the stage. Connor, on the other hand, looked like he'd just been punched. All his scheming to win king and here he was a lowly prince. I would have felt sorry for him, but I knew at the end of the night he'd be going home with his one true love anyway: himself.

"And last but not least, I'd like to introduce to you our Herbert Hoover High School homecoming king and queen . . ." She paused, pulling her glasses up to read the names.

The entire school leaned forward as one, waiting to hear the announcement.

"Well, look at that. It's a write-in couple. Samantha Kramer and Kyle Lowe!"

"Ohmigod!" Sam jumped up next to me, grabbing my arm in a vice grip. "Ohmigod. Ohmigod . . . Did you hear that? I think she called my name. Ohmigod!" She squealed so loud I thought I might bust an eardrum as she danced from foot to foot and grabbed onto Kyle's lapels.

"Dude, we are, like, the hottest couple in school!" Kyle said.

"Ohmigod! Ohmigod!"

I couldn't help smiling as I watched Sam and Kyle run up the stairs to the stage amid a roar of applause from the crowd to receive their crowns. Kyle's was a short, sparkling thing that looked like it belonged in a kid's dress-up box, and Sam's rivaled anything I'd ever seen on *Toddlers & Tiaras*, standing a good two feet above her natural hair.

Last year's queen put a sash over Sam's head, and Kyle and Sam held hands, grinning from ear to ear as the crowd cheered.

"Congratulations, Samantha and Kyle," Mrs. Bailey said into the microphone again. Though above the roar of the crowd still clapping, it was almost a lost cause. "Now we'd love to have all the couples on the dance floor join our king and queen in their first royal dance."

Slow music erupted from the speakers, a soft Jason Mraz song. The crowd settled down, dispersing, as people paired into twos, standing close to each other and swaying back and forth. Sam and Kyle descended the stage stairs and took up a spot in the center of the dance floor, one hand on each other, the other on their massive crowns to keep them from falling off.

I turned to go find another glass of Mango Madness when I felt Chase's hand on my arm.

"Hey. Where are you going?"

I glanced at the dance floor. "Well, it's only for couples."

Chase raised an eyebrow at me. "You are my date."

I blinked at him, trying to figure out if he was joking.

He grinned, a lopsided thing that showed off a dimple

in his left cheek. "Come on. Dance with me, Featherstone."

I pursed my lips together, tasting lipstick. "Okay. I guess."

Chase took my hand in his, and I instantly felt goose bumps break out, shivering down my bare arms. Must have been a sudden gust of wind. Certainly couldn't have anything to do with how warm his hands felt. How strong. How intimate.

Yep. Just the wind.

I gulped down a wave of apprehension as Chase moved in close, putting both hands at my waist. His palms were so hot, I was sure they were making smoldering handprints there. I ignored the sensation, focusing on moving my feet a few inches at a time to the left, letting Chase lead me in slow circles as we swayed with the rest of the couples.

"I like the dress," Chase said, his voice low. "Red's a good color on you."

I opened my mouth to speak, but only a strangled sort of squeak came out. I cleared my throat and tried again. "Uh, thanks. You . . . you look nice, too."

He grinned, that dimple making an appearance again. "Thanks. I feel kinda ridiculous in this, to be honest."

I shook my head. "No, you look good. It looks good on you. I mean, it's all good."

His smile widened. "Good."

And then he moved in closer, getting rid of any space

that might have existed between us, his arms going around my middle, his cheek close to mine, his breath heavy on my hair.

My entire body was suddenly filled with awkward energy. Was I stepping on his feet? Was my deodorant holding up okay? Where was I supposed to put my hands? I suddenly had to concentrate on the simplest of tasks. Like breathing. I inhaled the spicy scent of what was definitely cologne this time.

"Relax," Chase whispered in my ear as if he could read my racing mind. "I don't bite." He paused. "Unless you want me to."

Oh boy.

I stumbled, tripping over his foot, and twisting my ankle beneath my too-high heels.

Chase caught me. "Dude, I was kidding," he said, teeth showing as he grinned at me.

I nodded. "Right. Yeah. I know."

"You okay?"

"Great. Fine. Dandy. Just . . . it's a little warm. I'm gonna go hit the bathroom."

"Okay, I'll come with you," he said, grabbing my hand again.

I quickly pulled it back. "I think I can manage by myself."

"I'll walk you there."

"I'm fine. Geez! I'm just going to pee, okay?"

He paused. But instead of looking hurt, he just grinned again. "Okay. Go 'pee.' I'll wait here."

"Thank you."

I quickly scuttled from the dance floor, ducking my head so that my red cheeks didn't telegraph the mix of sensations rolling around in my belly right now. God, what was wrong with me? Clearly the tiara was cutting off circulation to my brain.

At the back of the cafeteria was a short hallway that ended in both the girls' and boys' bathrooms. At the moment it was nearly empty, since most of the school was out on the floor slow dancing.

While I needed a few minutes to get away from the heat, the truth was I did have to pee. Being nervous did that to me. And dancing with Chase had made me way nervous.

I turned down the corridor and made a beeline toward the bathroom.

But I never made it to that blue cutout of a girl figure on the door.

Instead, I felt something come at me from behind, a blinding pain erupting behind my right ear as bright spots danced in front of my face. The ground rushed up to meet me, my heels buckling under my feet, as the world went black.

TWENTY-TWO

THE FIRST THING I NOTICED WHEN I WOKE UP WAS THE HIPPO squatting on my head. Or at least that's what I assumed was happening based on the pressure building to a blinding pain between my ears. I took several beats, slowly breathing in and out, willing the hippo to go away before venturing to open my eyes. I slowly blinked one, then the other open, cringing through the pain.

It was dark. A faint glow from somewhere just outside my field of vision was the only light illuminating the area. I realized I was outside, a cool breeze whipping over my bare arms and making me shiver. It smelled faintly of chlorine, making me think I was near a swimming pool. I could hear faint sounds in the distance—crickets, music, the rumble of the freeway.

I blinked a few more times, slowly letting my senses

come alive again, and realized I did not, in fact, have a large water mammal on my head, just a really bad headache. I guess being brained from behind will do that to you.

I wriggled my hands and fingers as I tried to get my bearings, and quickly realized I didn't have much wiggle room at all. My hands were tied together behind my back. Ditto my feet. Whoever had hit me over the head had done a bang-up job of making sure I couldn't respond in kind.

As my eyes adjusted to the dark, I could see a metal utility shed in front of me, and the outline of the top of the math building. I was at the school. If I had to guess, near the swim team's pool.

And the faint glow of light I'd seen was coming from underneath the door of the utility shed. Someone was inside.

I moved left, then right, then realized not only were my hands and feet tied up, but I was tied to something. I craned my head around in the dark, coming up against a starting block. I wriggled back and forth. The bonds at my wrists were some sort of rope, strong and tightly knotted. No way was I going to break them before whoever was in the shed came back. I kicked my legs, twisting, but it was no use. I was stuck there.

And even worse?

The door to the utility shed was slowly opening.

I held my breath, watching as a shadowy figure backlit by the shed emerged. I blinked against the onslaught of light, trying to make out features. But it wasn't until he shut the door again that I was able to see his face clearly.

I let out a sigh of relief so loud, I swear they heard me all the way in the cafeteria over the blare of the DJ.

"Mr. Tipkins!" I breathed. "Oh, thank God. You've got to help me. Someone hit me on the head and dragged me out here and tied me up, and I think they might have killed Sydney, though I'm not sure, but it's highly possible because I said I was gonna blow the whistle, but I'm not really, 'cause I don't know who they are, but if you untie me, we can find them, and we will know!"

I paused for breath, taking in a big gulp of chlorine-tinted air, ignoring the pain at the sound of my own voice echoing through my throbbing head.

Mr. Tipkins took a step toward me.

I wriggled, showing him my bound wrists. "Can you see the knots?" I asked.

He nodded slowly. "Yes."

"Can you get them undone? Do they look too tight?"

"They look very tight," he responded, his voice flat.

"Well, there must be something in the utility shed sharp enough to cut these. A knife or scissors or something? I'm sure if you just go look . . ."

But I trailed off as I looked up at his face. It was calm

and impassive, definitely not the reaction you'd expect from someone finding a student tied up to a starting block in her homecoming dress.

Realization must have been plain in my eyes as my throbbing brain struggled to put the pieces together, because the corners of his mouth slowly turned upward, curving into a big wicked smile that showed off the coffee stains on his incisors in all their glory.

"You aren't going to untie me, are you?" I asked.

He shook his head slowly back and forth.

"Because you're the one who tied me up."

The grin grew wider as he nodded. "That's the first smart thing you've said, Miss Featherstone."

Dread hit my stomach in one swift punch. "You hit me over the head."

He crouched low, coming to eye level. "I did," he admitted.

"Just like you hit Nicky?"

He shrugged, palms upward.

"And you killed Sydney?"

"Sydney killed herself," he shot back, anger suddenly flashing through his eyes. "She was stupid and self-absorbed. That's what led to her downfall."

"But you're the one who committed Twittercide."

He frowned. "What?"

"Death by Twitter?"

He shook his head. "I don't know what you're talking about. I just pushed her into a pool."

Part of me did a happy dance that I finally knew who had killed Sydney. The other part of me, the more logical part, told me I was tied up and all alone with a killer who was confessing his crimes. That did not bode well for my future.

I looked past Mr. Tipkins to the school buildings beyond. I could hear the faint sounds of dance music coming from the cafeteria. It was so close, but a million miles away for all the good it did me. There was no way anyone could hear me scream from here. My calls for help would be swallowed up long before they could reach the partygoers, even if they didn't have top blast music drowning me out.

I was on my own.

With a murderer.

"Why did you kill her?" I asked. Not that finding out was my top priority at the moment. But the more time I could buy, the better chance someone might wander this way. Surely there was some couple at the dance who would go looking for a private corner to make out in, right? Possibly near the pool?

"Why?" Tipkins snorted. "That should be as obvious as any three noncollinear points on a two-dimensional flat surface."

I blinked at him. "Huh?"

Tipkins scowled. "A plane! God, don't you kids ever pay attention in class?"

I figured that question was rhetorical at this point.

"Fine," he said. "I'll spell it out for you. I had to shut Sydney up before she could tell everyone what was going on."

"And what was going on?" I asked, wriggling against my bonds. There was no way the rope was going to give out, but if I could possibly slip my hand through the loop . . .

"I should think that would be obvious. I was selling test answers."

"You!" I shook my head. "But why?" Honestly, I was genuinely curious. It seemed like the last thing a teacher would want.

"Why?" Tipkins repeated, his voice rising. "Why! Do you know how much I make babysitting ignorant brats like you?"

I bit my lip. There was no right answer to this question, was there?

Luckily, I didn't have to say anything as he continued his rant. "Hardly enough to survive on, that's how much. I have a PhD. I graduated at the top of my class from Cornell. I'm a damned math genius! And now I spend the majority of my life trying to figure out how to keep texting idiots from stealing test answers."

"So you decided to give the idiots the answers instead."

"Sell," he corrected me. "I'm finally getting what I'm worth. You idiot brats want to go to college? You go through me."

"So you sold the answers to your own tests?"

Tipkins nodded. "Mine and everyone else's. It was easy. I had access to anything I wanted in the teachers' lounge."

Mental face palm. All our breaking and entering had been for nothing. No wonder the thief hadn't worried about locks—he had a key all along!

"But why involve Nicky?" I asked, feeling my hand slip a scant quarter inch lower in the bonds. If I could work up enough sweat on my wrists, I might have a chance of slipping free.

"I couldn't very well risk the exposure of selling them myself, now, could I?" Tipkins answered. "I caught Nicky last year trying to cheat on one of my tests. It was one of the more sophisticated attempts I'd ever seen, I'll give him that. He had hacked into my email account and found a copy of the test answers that I'd sent to the administration for compliance with state standards. He'd memorized the answers completely, so there was no proof of anything in the classroom at all."

I wrinkled my forehead. "So how did you catch him?"

Tipkins grinned, satisfaction at outsmarting a teen clear on his face. "I gave a different test that day. At the last minute, the vice principal had told me they hadn't gotten the go-ahead from the state on the standards yet, and I ended up giving the old test. Nicky got every single question wrong, but I quickly realized why."

"And you recruited him to work for you?"

Tipkins shrugged. "I simply told him he could either make a small percentage working for me or I would tell the vice principal I'd caught him cheating."

"So you blackmailed him?"

Tipkins frowned, his eyes going dark again. "Don't make it sound like he was innocent here. He was a cheater!"

"Just like Sydney?" I asked. My right wrist had gone as far as I could slip it, so I started wriggling my left as Tipkins nodded in agreement.

"Yes. That's right. Only Nicky was smart. Sydney was a moron. It was like she wanted to get caught. Answers on her fingernails?" he asked, waving his own grubby set in my face. "How obvious can you get? Every student within a three-desk radius saw what she was doing. I had to bust her. How could I not? I had no choice."

"But weren't you worried she was going to blow the whistle on you?"

"What whistle? She had no idea who I was." He paused. "Until you started asking questions."

I gulped. "Me?" I squeaked out.

He nodded. "As soon as you started nosing around,

Sydney did, too. She knew the school board was investigating and realized how badly everyone wanted to know how the answers had gotten out. She bribed Nicky to tell her who was giving him the cheats, then she called me and said that if I didn't get her reinstated on the homecoming court she was going to tell the administration all about it."

I nodded. The blackmailer becomes the blackmailee. Nice move. I had to say, it didn't sound like Sydney was as dumb as Mr. Tipkins had thought after all.

"That's why she agreed to meet with me?"

Tipkins nodded. "She said if I didn't get her back on the court, she was going to tell you everything and it would be all over the paper."

"But you couldn't let that happen."

He shook his head slowly back and forth. "No. I had too much of a good thing going. I was finally making good money. I wasn't going to let some no-brained bimbo take that away from me."

"So you went to her house?"

He nodded. "After you came to interview me, I realized I couldn't let her talk to you. So I went to her house. She was in the backyard, tanning of all things! Made suspension look more like a vacation than a punishment to me."

"And she had her laptop with her?"

He nodded. "Plugged into an outlet. She was on the damned Titter on her laptop."

"Twitter," I corrected automatically.

"Whatever. She was too busy on that thing to even listen to me. I tried to tell her I didn't have the authority to get her back on the homecoming court. I told her I'd pay her off, make it worth her while to keep her mouth shut."

"But she didn't go for it?"

"She said all she cared about was being homecoming queen."

"So you killed her?"

He nodded, an eerie light in his eyes. "It was easy. All I had to do was give her a little shove, and into the pool she went."

"With her laptop," I pointed out.

He grinned, showing off those grotesquely stained teeth again.

I shivered, imagining how her last moments must have been. Had she felt the electric shock? Felt the water flowing into her paralyzed lungs? Or had she died instantly, one minute here and the next just . . . not?

"And now . . . ," Mr. Tipkins said, taking a step toward me, "it's time to tie up the last little loose end."

Oh, fantastic amounts of fluffin' fudge.

TWENTY-THREE

I WATCHED IN HORROR AS MR. TIPKINS'S EYES CHANGED. Gone was the angry flash when he'd talked about how he was an underpaid, underappreciated teacher, the confusion of trying to figure out Titter versus Twitter, and the disdain when he'd spoken about the ignorance of his current students. This was something different. Something dead, flat, and calm, and more eerily menacing than anything I'd ever seen.

Anxiety balled into pure panic in my stomach, making my body move and squirm all on its own.

"Um, you know what? I'm no loose end. I'm hardly an end at all. You see, I'm not into being homecoming queen, or getting cash, or anything like that. I'm totally just into being quiet. Not talking. Not telling anyone about anything. I can be totally quiet, see?" I shut my mouth illustrating my point.

Tipkins shook his head. He was so not buying this.

And I was so out of time.

I wriggled my wrists as he rounded the starting block, coming up behind me. The left one slipped a little. I'd worked out some slack in the rope. But it still held tight.

"You won't get away with this," I said, changing tactics. "Someone will notice I'm gone. They'll come looking for me."

Speaking of which—where the heck was Chase? How long would he wait before realizing I wasn't just in the bathroom? How long had I been out? How long would it take him to figure out I was here, on campus still, by the pool with a Twittercidal maniac?

Though, I realized as Mr. Tipkins began to separate my bound wrists from the board, it didn't matter. I was out of time altogether.

"What are you going to do?" I asked, my voice shaking.

He didn't answer, instead pulling me up off the ground by my still-bound-together hands. I tried to struggle out of his grasp, but for someone who spent the majority of his life sitting behind a desk, he was surprisingly strong. And, as he steered me toward the edge of the pool, a horrific realization dawned on me.

He was going to throw me in.

"Wait, you can't do this," I said, doing my best to

dig my heels into the cement. "Please, I swear I won't tell anyone what you've been up to."

"Too late," Tipkins said, his hands gripping both my arms as he pushed me forward.

I did the only thing I could think of. I went limp, playing noncompliant toddler and sagging to the ground at the side of the pool.

"Help!" I yelled, being dead weight to the best of my abilities. "Help! Someone help me!"

"No one can hear you," Tipkins said, towering over me, hands on his ample hips. "They're all enjoying their stupid dance."

Which is where, more than anything, I wanted to be. Dancing, laughing. Where I'd been just a few minutes ago now felt an entire world away. Had that been the last time I'd ever see my friends? Sam and Kyle? Chase?

"Help!" I screamed at the top of my lungs. Even though I knew Tipkins was right—there was no way my volume could compete with the DJ's. No one would hear me. No one would run to the rescue.

I was on my own. And if I was going to get out of this alive, I was going to have to save myself.

Mr. Tipkins leaned down, putting both hands under my armpits to lift me off the ground.

It was now or never.

I took a deep breath . . .

. . . and head-butted him in the nose as hard as I could.

"Unh!" Mr. Tipkins reeled backward, his hands going to his face.

I took the opportunity to pop up to my feet, hopping like a bunny toward the gate that encircled the pool. Only, since Tipkins had two separated feet, he quickly recovered and caught up to me. I felt him shove at my back, hard enough that we both fell to the ground.

I rolled to the right, bringing my feet up and kicking as hard as I could, catching him squarely in the chest. I heard the wind whoosh out of his lungs. I inchwormed myself into a sitting position, pulling my legs under me to awkwardly get back on my feet.

I got one hop away before Tipkins's hairy-knuckled hand grabbed the rope at my ankles, pulling me backward and down to the ground again.

I fell hard, both knees scraping against the cement as I landed with a thud that jarred my teeth together. I wriggled and kicked backward with both feet as hard as I could, connecting with something soft and fleshy.

Tipkins grunted but kept a hand on my ankles.

"Let. Go. Of. Me!" I shouted.

"Not on your life," he growled back, regaining his breath and pulling himself onto his knees.

Right at the edge of the pool.

I scrunched myself up into a fetal position, cocking my

knees as close to my chest as I could, then shoved hard with both feet.

My extra-high heels caught Tipkins in the stomach, doubling him over in the middle. I kicked again, connecting with his forehead and watched as he toppled backward, hitting the water with a splash that sent water sloshing over the side of the pool.

I didn't waste any time, immediately popping to my feet, kicking off the heels, and hopping toward the gate again.

I heard Tipkins splashing around in the water. His clothes slowed him down, but it wouldn't be long before he found his way to the side and out onto dry land again. I had to move fast.

I hopped as quickly as I could, only vaguely aware of how ridiculous I must have looked, making it to the side gate just as I heard Tipkins sloshing up the ladder and out of the pool.

I pushed on the gate, but it was firmly latched in place. Not only that, but a shiny, silver lock gleamed back at me in the moonlight.

I felt desperation bubble up in my throat as I whipped my head around for any sign of a key. But it was too late. I could hear Tipkins's wet footsteps moving the length of the pool. In an instant, his arms encircled me from behind, wet, rigid, and as unyielding as steel.

"No!" I cried out, feeling tears well in my eyes as he dragged me toward the water.

"Please, I—"

But that was as far as I got in my pleading because, without ceremony, Tipkins tossed me over the edge, into the deep end of the pool.

Cold water instantly enveloped me, hitting my body like a shock. I kicked my legs, wiggled from side to side, moving anything I could as the frigid water rushed over my body, pressing in on me from all sides as I sank lower and lower.

I felt panic coursing through my system and fought the urge to scream as I watched the surface of the pool grow farther and farther away. I could just make out the blurry figure of Mr. Tipkins walking away.

Leaving me there to drown in a watery grave.

I felt hot tears slide down my cheeks in the freezing water. I thrashed, the ropes cutting into my wrists until they burned like they were on fire. I kicked, my feet coming up against something hard. The bottom of the pool. I shoved with all my might, shooting toward the surface . . . but I fell short, only managing to move a couple feet through the thick water . . . that felt like it was growing thicker and heavier by the second, pressing in on me, closing my visions down to one small pinpoint of light as my eyes grew heavy. My lungs were screaming for air, burning, feeling as if they were going to burst at any second. I wasn't sure how much longer I could resist the urge to open my mouth, not drag the heavily chlorinated water into my body, filling my lungs until I drowned.

My brain began to feel fuzzy, images swimming in my vision as I watched the last of my oxygen leak out of my nose in tiny little air bubbles that floated so easily to the surface. If only I could float like that. If only I was light enough to just float right out of my body, up toward the surface out into that sweet, sweet air.

And suddenly I was floating. I vaguely wondered if maybe I'd left my body, if I was dead and floating toward the heavens, slowly rising from the water. I watched the surface swim closer and closer until I could almost feel the crisp breeze of gloriously fresh air.

I opened my mouth, not able to hold it in any longer, sucking in as hard as I could, expecting the rush of water to fill my lungs and end it all.

Only it didn't.

Instead, I dragged in a deep, full breath of air as my body broke the surface.

I gasped, coughing, choking, and dragging in oxygen as if I couldn't get enough.

"Hartley!" I heard someone calling my name from very far away.

But I didn't care. All I cared about was the delicious

feeling of filling my lungs, in and out, in and out. Was there anything better?

"Hartley? Can you hear me?" the voice pressed.

I blinked, regaining my vision, the oxygen slowly clearing the clouds from my brains. A face came into focus in front of me. A heavily made-up face, surrounded by clouds of blond hair.

"Drea?" I asked, confusion lacing my voice as her features materialized in front of me.

"Ohmigod, you're okay!" She leaned down and hugged me, my soggy self making wet spots on her itty-bitty minidress.

"What are you doing here?" I asked.

"Rescuing you," came another voice. I looked to my right and saw two more cheerleaders from Drea's posse standing nearby.

"We saw everything," Drea said. "We came running to get you out as soon as we could." I looked down and saw a long pole with a hook on the end that the maintenance workers used to drag leaves from the bottom of the pool. Or in this case, cheerleaders used to drag me from the bottom of the pool.

Great. Saved by cheerleaders. I would never live this down.

"Thanks," I said. "But how did you find me?" I asked, still dragging in deep breaths.

"We were shooting videos of the dance for Nicky," Drea explained, leaning down to untie my bonds.

"And we saw Mr. Tipkins helping you from the girls' bathroom," Cheerleader number one said. "We totally thought you were drunk or something."

"Yeah, so we followed you guys, shooting in case you puked or something cool," Cheerleader number two said.

"Nicky would have loved that," Drea agreed.

I just bet.

"But I wasn't drunk," I pointed out.

Drea nodded. "Yeah, we realized that when he tied you up."

I blinked at her. "You watched him tie me up? Why didn't you help me?"

"Dude, we tried! The gate was locked, and we couldn't get in."

"We even tried to climb over the fence," Cheerleader number one said, "but that totally wasn't working with our wardrobes." She gestured to the micromini dresses they all wore.

Drea nodded in agreement. "It wasn't until Tipkins opened the gate and left that we could get in and rescue you."

"Thanks," I told them. Meaning it. If it hadn't been for them hoping to catch me making a fool of myself, I'd have made a dead body of myself. "And Mr. Tipkins?" I asked, my gaze whipping around the area.

"He ran," number two said. "Totally took off toward the parking lot as soon as he tossed you."

"So he got away?" I asked, a sinking feeling hitting my stomach.

But Drea grinned. "Not for long. I got his whole confession on video." She held up the Flip cam she'd been carrying around with her all night. "And," she added, hitting a little red button on the side, "it's all uploading to YouTube as we speak."

I grinned.

Score one for the brats and their technology.

TWENTY-FOUR

TWENTY MINUTES LATER, IT SEEMED LIKE THE ENTIRE STUDENT population of Herbert Hoover High was standing by the pool, plus our chaperones, teachers, and about a dozen police officers. Drea and Cheerleaders number one and two were enthusiastically giving their statements to officers, complete with lots of hand waving, jumping up and down, and video footage of them coming to my rescue. Sam and Kyle were exactly where they'd been ever since running from the cafeteria at speeds that left both crowns at odd angles: right by my side. Sam had immediately wrapped both arms around me, letting go only when I begged for air, and hadn't let go of my hand since. Kyle had taken it upon himself to shield me from the thousand questions everyone began throwing at me the second they saw my dripping hair and soggy homecoming dress, holding them at bay by repeatedly yelling, "Give her some room to breathe!"

Someone had found a tarp in the utility shed, which I'd wrapped around myself as a makeshift blanket, but I was still shivering through my wet clothes as I sat on the ground beside the pool. "Hartley!" I heard a voice call through the crowd, and looked up to find Chase rushing toward me. He ignored the crowd, police, and chaperones, enveloping me in a hug so fierce, I might have mistaken him for Mom.

I'll admit, with his arms around me, some warmth started to return to my system.

"God, I've been looking everywhere for you," he said when he finally pulled away. "As soon as I saw you were gone, I texted everyone to see if they'd seen you. Ashley said she thought she saw you heading toward the quad, Chris said he thought you went out to the parking lot, Jenni said to try the football field. I've been all over the school looking." He ran a hand through his hair, and I could tell by the way his spikes stood up in messy tufts that it hadn't been the first time he'd done it that evening. His face was pale in the moonlight, his mouth drawn in a tight line. He really did look like he'd been worried.

More of that welcome warmth pooled in my stomach at the thought.

"I'm okay," I reassured him. Though "okay" was kind

of a relative term at the moment. But I was alive, and that was a lot more than I might have hoped for earlier.

I quickly told him everything, from being hit on the head to being rescued by Drea and company. I was just finishing when I saw another familiar face push through the crowd. Freckled, slightly wrinkled, and topped with red hair.

Raley.

And behind him trailed Mom, pushing her way toward me.

"Oh, Hartley," she said, grabbing me around the middle.

I hugged her back. After the night I'd had, I could use all the hugs I could get.

When she finally pulled away, I noticed for the first time what she was wearing. And it was not the yoga pants and T-shirt I'd left her in earlier that evening.

It was a black sleeveless dress that ended well above her knee, paired with heels that were higher than mine.

"Why are you all dressed up?" I asked.

She looked down. "Well, David and I were at dinner when he got the call about you."

I cocked my head to the side. "David?"

She blushed. "Detective Raley."

Mental face palm.

My gaze shifted to Raley and I noticed he was also a notch up from his usual schlumpy fare, wearing a pair of dark slacks with a shirt that actually looked cleaned and ironed.

That's it. This was getting out of hand.

"This is the third date in as many days, Mom."

"I know." She beamed. "Well, technically, it might be the fourth, since David was at our house so late last night—"

"Oh God, Mom. Please stop talking now."

She shot me a look but, considering my near-death experience, was thankfully compassionate enough to comply.

After giving another quick version of events to Raley (no way was I ever going to think of him as "David"), he told Mom she could take me home and he'd come over tomorrow to take down an official statement.

Then Mom bundled me into her minivan, cranked the heat to full blast, and took me home, where I took the longest, hottest shower on record. (But not a bath. I wasn't sure I wanted to go near standing water ever again.)

Afterward, I slipped into a pair of long johns, a pair of sweats, two pairs of socks, and fluffy pink slippers, and I was almost warm again.

Mom made me a cup of hot cocoa (with soy milk and organic fructose), though I was so tired, I could hardly hold my head up to sip at it before I fell into bed, my eyes closing almost before I even hit the pillows.

HERBERT HOOVER HIGH TEACHER ARRESTED FOR MURDER

Long known as one of the toughest teachers on campus, Mr. Tipkins was arrested Saturday evening for the murder of HHH student Sydney Sanders, as well as the attempted murders of both Nicky Williams and yours truly, Hartley Grace Featherstone. Mr. Tipkins has pled not guilty but, due to an inability to post bail, was remanded to the county detention facility, pending trial.

The arrest was on the heels of a video of Mr. Tipkins confessing to his crimes that circulated on YouTube. Incidentally the video received 550,000 hits in the first weekend, making it YouTube's top video of the week.

I looked down at my article. I had to admit, it wasn't bad. Unfortunately, the major media outlets had gotten hold of the story before I'd had a chance to break the news in the *Homepage*, but I had the most unique angle there was—from a survivor of Mr. Tipkins's attack. Which included both my perspective on the matter and a whole host of juicy inside facts. And, as Chase had wanted, this was definitely an angle no one else had heard on the story of Sydney's death.

Which, after viewing Tipkins's confession, Raley had reopened the case files on, changing the official ruling from suicide to homicide. (Sam and I couldn't quite convince him to put "Twittercide" in the official report.) He and his police force had found Mr. Tipkins at home, where he'd been packing his bags for Mexico. Into the trunk of his Toyota. Which gave Raley enough probable cause to charge him with not one but two attempts on my life.

And while the extra paperwork had tied Raley up for the day, he'd still found time to go out with my mom again the following evening. I was seriously working on a plan to stop this before it got out of hand. As if living with the SMother wasn't enough, now a cop was invading my life, too. Not cool. Way not cool.

As for our suspects . . . Nicky was released from the hospital the day after homecoming, but after Tipkins's cheating scheme was exposed, the administration had no choice but to suspend Nicky for his part in it. Since Nicky currently had a 4.0 GPA, rumor had it he wasn't really worried about the blemish on his record. And Drea had promised to shoot videos for him of everything he missed at school.

The person who had taken news of Sydney's death most definitely not being a suicide the hardest was Connor. The fact that no one actually thought him worth killing themselves over had been a blow I wasn't sure his ego would ever recover from. Well, at least not until the winter formal.

Jenni, on the other hand, was already working on a

nomination for homecoming queen next year. According to Ashley Stannic's gossip column, Jenni was back together with Ben Fisher, and the two of them were seen wearing matching his and hers shirts to the mall last weekend.

Quinn Leslie had been allowed back on the lacrosse team, pending academic probation. Incidentally, she was the only one still wearing a black mourning armband for her best friend. She'd even tried to get a scholarship fund going in Sydney's name.

And, as a minor last note, I'm proud to say that both Sam and I did pass our American Government midterm. Sam even got the highest grade in the class, completely ruining the grading curve for everyone else. Without cheating. Poor Chris Fret got a 65, but Sam gave him the name of her tutor, so I'm sure he'll be bringing up his grades soon.

"You got that article, Featherstone?" Chase asked, coming up behind me in the workroom.

I nodded. "Yep. Just emailed it to you."

"Cool," he said. But instead of walking away, he sat down at the desk beside me.

"Um, did you want to read it right now?"

He shook his head. "No, that's fine. I'll read it later."

I waited a beat, but he just sat there.

"Was there something else?" I asked, starting to feel a little self-conscious.

He cleared his throat, his fingers picking at a piece of lint on his black hoodie. "Actually, yeah. I, uh, I wanted to apologize."

I cocked my head at him. "For?"

He swallowed, his Adam's apple bobbing up and down. "For leaving you alone at the dance. For letting Tipkins attack you like that."

I shook my head. "That wasn't your fault."

"I was supposed to be watching you."

"Watching me pee? Come on. You couldn't follow me everywhere."

He shrugged. "I should have stayed closer."

"It wasn't your fault. And I totally don't blame you."

He looked up at me through his eyelashes. "You sure?"

I nodded, feeling my hair bob around my ears. "Totally."

"So, we're cool?"

"Cool."

"Good." He let out a sigh, the corners of his mouth turning up. "In that case . . ." He cleared his throat again, eyes going back to his hoodie lint. "I was wondering what you were doing this Friday."

I shrugged. "No plans. Why?"

"Well, I was kinda wondering if you wanted to hang out. Maybe get some pizza or something."

I paused. "Like another *Homepage* staff meeting thing?"

"Not really," he said, eyes still on the lint.

"Is this about a story? A new assignment or something?" I pressed.

"No."

"Then what?"

He shrugged. "I just thought that maybe you'd like to go grab something to eat. You know. With me."

I narrowed my eyes. "Are you asking me out?"

I didn't think it was possible, but I swear I saw Chase's cheeks go just the slightest pale shade of pink.

"Sorta. Yeah. I guess. I mean, if you want to."

I paused. Did I want to?

"What about that girl you were at the game with last week?" I hedged.

Chase finally lifted his eyes from the lint ball to meet mine, his eyebrows scrunching. "Carly?"

I swallowed. "Yeah. Carly."

"What about her?"

"Um, don't you think she'd mind you going out with me?" I asked.

But my sarcasm was lost on him, his eyebrows still scrunching. "Why would my cousin mind me having pizza with you?"

I blinked. His cousin.

Dude, I was so stupid.

"Your cousin. Carly."

Chase shook his head. "So, what do you say? You, me, pizza? Sound like fun?" A lopsided grin broke through the deepening pink in his cheeks, his eyes warm and soft in a way that inexplicably made my insides feel warm and soft, too.

And I felt myself nodding.

"Sure. Pizza."

Pizza was good, I told myself. Pizza was easy. Friends had pizza all the time. We were good friends having pizza on a Friday night. It didn't need to mean anything more than that, and I was definitely not reading anything more into it.

For now.

Chase grinned wide enough that white teeth showed between his lips. "Awesome," he said. Then he finally did get up from the desk, taking a step toward the door before he called over his shoulder, "It's a date, then."

Oh, fluffin' fudge. Was Sam gonna have a field day with this one.